LOST AND DROWNED

A BELLBROOK MURDER MYSTERY

REAGAN DAVIS

COPYRIGHT

ISBN: 978-1-990228-54-4 (ebook)

ISBN: 978-1-990228-55-1 (paperback)

ISBN: 978-1-990228-56-8 (hardcover)

ISBN: 978-1-990228-57-5 (large print)

FOREWORD

Dear Reader,

Despite several layers of editing and proofreading, occasionally a typo or grammar mistake is so stubborn that it manages to thwart my editing efforts and camouflage itself amongst the words in the book.

If you encounter one of these obstinate typos or errors in this book, please let me know by contacting me at Hello@ReaganDavis.com.

Hopefully, together we can exterminate the annoying pests.

Thank you!

Reagan Davis

CONTENTS

ONE

THE AQUAHOLIC

THE DAY of the murder

Karla inhaled a lungful of salty sea air and fixed her eyes on the hazy grey-blue horizon line in the distance. The blurry boundary between ocean and sky that she could see but never touch, chase but never catch. Elusive. Limitless and untouchable. She loved that horizon line. It was her favourite part of the ocean. It drew her eye more than the waves, and even more than the whales that sometimes surfaced in the distance.

"Thanks for the lift," she said to her sister, Max. "The dealership said my car should be ready this afternoon."

"I don't mind driving you around," Max said, adjusting one of the many zips and pockets on her police vest. "Besides, it's not every day I get to see a yacht up close."

The Aquaholic wasn't exactly close. It was too big to

dock near shore, so it sat anchored out in the ocean, a man-made floating refuge. There was nothing discreet or understated about it. The ship was massive, white, and covered with mirrored windows that gleamed in the sun. The points of light reflecting off the water made the vessel sparkle like a diamond in a jewellery store.

"It's a mega yacht," Karla corrected. "My client was quite specific that it's a mega yacht."

"What's the difference?" Max slid her aviator sunglasses from the top of her head to her eyes, staring at the enormous ship. "A yacht's a yacht, right?"

"Size," Karla explained. "Apparently a mega yacht is bigger than a regular yacht."

"It's always about size," Max said with a sigh and a headshake.

The sisters laughed.

"Here's my ride." Karla nodded toward the yacht tender that was cruising toward them. "I'll be onboard for about an hour," she said, checking the time on her phone.

"Text me when you're ready, and I'll pick you up."

Karla strode down the long pier to meet the tender. She turned and waved to Max.

Max waved back but didn't turn to leave.

Karla knew Max wouldn't leave until she had safely boarded the small watercraft, and it had sped away from the pier. Watching, protecting, helping, they were part of Max's nature. She couldn't stop herself.

"G'day!" The well-tanned, uniformed man had a deep voice with an Aussie lilt. "Welcome aboard." He extended his hand to help Karla step aboard the speedboat.

"Thank you." She slung her bag over her shoulder and gave him one hand while she used the other to lift the hem of her long sundress. A loose, flowy, maxi wrap-dress with an all-over floral pattern. "I'm Karla Bell." She smiled and stepped onto the boat, glad she'd opted for flats instead of the stiletto sandals she usually wore with this dress. "It's nice to meet you."

"Captain Henry Peterson." The man returned the smile.

Captain Peterson was a conventionally handsome man, tall and lean with a well-tailored white captain's uniform. His chiseled face was clean shaven, and a hint of salt and pepper hair peeked out from beneath his captain's hat. His deeply tanned skin made his teeth appear unnaturally white and exaggerated the smile lines around his mouth and eyes. Karla guesstimated he was about fifty years old and, judging by the thick band of gold on his left ring finger, married.

"Does the ship's captain usually ferry guests back and forth from the yacht?" Karla asked.

"No," Captain Peterson replied. "But everyone else was busy, and Mr. Casey said to treat you like a VIP." He gave her a quick grin. "No luggage?"

"I'm not staying," Karla shouted over the boat's motor and surrounding sea sounds.

"Well, Mr. Casey had a deluxe cabin prepared for you, in case you change your mind," bellowed Captain Peterson as he navigated away from the pier and aimed the boat toward The Aquaholic.

"That's very kind of him," Karla shouted over the ocean waves crashing against the bow of the speedboat. "But I only live about ten minutes from here." She steadied herself against the back of her tan leather seat with one hand and held her wide-brimmed sun hat in place with the other. The front of the brim curled and flapped against the headwind like it was trying to take flight. "And I have a dog. His name is Gucci. I hate to leave him." She wasn't sure if the captain didn't hear her or didn't care.

Karla stepped off the tender and boarded the yacht. She had barely finished thanking Captain Peterson when a tall, professional woman with a leather planner, cell phone, and the confident urgency of a Type-A personality whisked her away.

"Lovely to see you again, Karla." said the woman without breaking her brisk stride. "Welcome aboard. Am I correct that this is your first time visiting us on The Aquaholic?"

"Nice to see you again, as well, Caitlin." Karla smiled and did an awkward trot-jog to catch up to the rushing woman. Caitlin's long, willowy legs took longer strides than Karla's ever could. "Yes, this is my first time aboard. It's even more magnificent in person."

Caitlin Lopez was, in Karla's opinion, one of the most organized and efficient people who had ever lived. Coming from Karla, who prided herself on organization and efficiency, that was quite a compliment. Caitlin was the embodiment of productivity from her no-nonsense chin-length tonal-brown bob to her ever-present leather-bound planner, and her fitted lilac power suit that featured crisp walking shorts in lieu of a skirt or pants. Karla had been tempted, more than once, to let Caitlin discreetly know that, should she ever find herself between jobs, Karla would love to hire her as a concierge at Just Task Me! But Caitlin had been Damien Casey's executive assistant for twenty years. She seemed content and well-compensated, so it was unlikely that she'd be interested in a concierge position. Why change jobs when she got to live on a luxury yacht and travel the world?

They hurried along narrow corridors and turned several corners before climbing a few steps and emerging onto a large white deck that was decorated like an outdoor living room.

"Have a seat." Caitlin gestured with her phone hand to the cushioned furniture arrangement near the outdoor bar. "Can I offer you a drink? We have a fully stocked bar, and we make our lemonade and iced tea fresh throughout the day."

"I would love an iced tea. Thank you," Karla said graciously.

Caitlin gave a terse nod to the crew member behind the bar.

He sprang into action, scooping ice into a large tumbler he had produced from somewhere beneath the bar.

"Mr. Casey will be with you shortly," Caitlin advised. "In the meantime, if you need anything, the deckhand will help you."

"Thanks, Caitlin." Karla smiled and removed her sunhat. She smoothed her hands along her blonde hair, ensuring no flyaways had escaped from the low, sleek chignon during the short, blustery speedboat ride.

Caitlin left the deck and disappeared down the steps that led to the underbelly of the enormous yacht.

The deckhand placed Karla's iced tea on the table next to her on top of a custom cocktail napkin branded with the yacht's name, The Aquaholic, in a cartoonish blue font that resembled ocean waves.

She thanked him, and as she reached over to pick up the insulated tumbler, Damien Casey strode onto the deck flanked by his daughter, her fiancé, and an air of superiority.

Damian Casey was an average-sized man with an above-average presence. He took up most of the air in every room he entered, even when that room was a wide-open deck in the middle of the Atlantic Ocean. He looked like an advertisement for nautical casual wear, dressed in a pair of white walking shorts with a brown leather belt and coordinating brown leather deck shoes.

His signature Cuban cigar was in his right hand—unlit—and he had another at the ready in the breast pocket of his loose fitting, light blue button-down shirt. His shirt sleeves were rolled up to his elbows, and the shirt was mostly unbuttoned, revealing a thick patch of chest hair that was much darker than the shaggy sand-coloured hair on his head.

"Good afternoon, Karla." His southern drawl elongated the last syllable of each word. "Welcome aboard my humble abode." He smiled and raised his dark sunglasses, nesting them in his hair. "If you need anything to make your visit more comfortable, you just let me know." He stepped forward and extended a hand.

"That's my line," Karla teased, standing up and shaking her client's hand. "I'm here to make *your* life as easy as possible."

Karla's concierge business, Just Task Me! specialized in catering to the whims and fancies of affluent clients like Damien Casey. People whose exclusive lifestyles were highly visible but inaccessible to all but an elite few. Most of Karla's clients ran Fortune 500 companies, were self-made tech millionaires, celebrities, or aristocratic types with generational wealth. However, Damien Casey was none of the above. He'd never run a company, as far as Karla knew. He'd never innovated anything techy, entertained anyone, or inherited his wealth. Damien Casey was a lobbyist. Without ever running for public office, he had politicked his way into a lucrative and successful career in foreign affairs and international politics. His ability to socialize, influence, and broker alliances had made him a very wealthy, very well-connected man. Karla chose to ignore the rumours of blackmail, manipulation, and influence peddling that seemed to follow Damien Casey around like a bad smell.

"This is my daughter, Saskia." He placed the unlit cigar between his teeth and gestured to his daughter.

"We've met online," Karla shook Saskia's hand. "It's wonderful to meet you in person, Saskia."

"Daddy, Karla and I have been exchanging emails and video calls while she helps me and Ben find the perfect wedding venue," Saskia explained to her father.

Saskia did not have the same southern drawl as Damien. In fact, she had no discernible accent at all. Her father was from the American deep south, and her mother was a 1990s German-born supermodel-turned-socialite and recovering addict, who now divided her time between New York and London. Damien and Saskia's mother never married. Saskia was the product of a short, tumultuous relationship that ended with a highly publicized custody battle and tell-all book written by her former nanny. Damien won the custody battle, of course. Damien Casey always got what he wanted. Saskia was raised by him, a team of the best nannies money could buy, and the most prestigious all-girl boarding schools on the East Coast.

Saskia was a mix of both her parents. She had

inherited her mother's angular bone structure and thick dark hair, as well as her father's light amber eyes and charisma.

"This is my fiancé, Ben Underwood." Saskia stood aside, making room for Ben to step forward.

"Nice to meet you, ma'am." He extended his hand and gave Karla a thousand-watt smile.

"Please, call me Karla."

"Yes, ma'am." He chuckled. "I mean yes, Karla."

Ben was more reserved than his photogenic fiancée and her charismatic father. He was attractive for someone his age.

Having just turned forty, men Ben's age—mid-to-late twenties—had fallen off Karla's radar, but she could still appreciate his fit physique, youthful glow, short, trendy black frohawk, dark smouldering eyes, and the two days of stubble that adorned his chin. Ben had been an up-and-coming football star, but an unfortunate career-ending knee injury sidelined his career early on.

"I can't wait to visit the venue." Saskia stretched out on a chaise lounge, kicked off her black wedge heels, and caught the deckhand's eye, wordlessly indicating that she would like a drink. Her gauzy white cover-up was transparent enough to make out the silhouette of the black cut out swimsuit underneath.

Ben sat on the chaise next to her, and Damien joined Karla on the generous loveseat.

Without taking their orders, the deckhand delivered a tray of drinks and served each of them.

"So, tell me about this venue," Damien said, then ran the length of his unlit cigar under his nose, inhaling its essence.

"Well, Bellcroft is my ancestral home," Karla began.

She gave her clients a brief history of Bellcroft and its local significance. Bellcroft was the name of the estate, composed of a sizable plot of oceanside property, a large manor house—the potential wedding venue—two small cottages—Mirabel and Bellflower—and a gamekeeper's cabin in the woods.

"And no one else has ever been married there?" Saskia asked. Again. Like she did every time she discussed wedding venues with Karla.

"No one in living memory," Karla clarified. "My grandparents and great-grandparents were married on the grounds, but to the best of my knowledge, the estate hasn't hosted any other weddings. Certainly not in the past sixty years."

"It's very important to Saskia that she and Ben get married somewhere special," Damien explained as he opened a plain wooden box on the coffee table and pulled out a box of matches. "She's a bit of a trendsetter, you see. She likes to be first." Damien struck a match and held the foot of the cigar close to the flame, rotating it as he toasted it.

Karla nodded as the proud father boasted.

Saskia Casey had turned trendsetting into an

empire. Thanks to the phenomenon known as social media, Saskia Casey™ was a luxury lifestyle brand. She had a PR team, glam squad, a team of stylists, a manager, and an agent. Saskia commanded a six-figure appearance fee for showing up at trendy nightclubs and star-studded after-parties. She was a social media influencer. Millions of followers around the globe—mostly young women—followed her every move and obsessed over her every post, endeavouring to copy her style, hoping to experience a teeny bit of Saskia's champagne-wishes-and-caviar-dreams lifestyle for themselves. Luxury brands competed to give her free samples and financial endorsements in exchange for a staged photo or short video of her using their products. When Saskia Casey endorsed a product, that product went viral and became The Next Big Thing.

"Will your wedding planner be joining us for the tour?" Karla asked.

Damien brought the smoldering cigar to his mouth and started puffing it, drawing the flame from the match toward the tip of the cigar.

"No." Saskia gave Ben a sideways glance. "We're not sure we want to continue using the wedding planner," she elaborated. "We're hoping, if we choose Bellcroft as the venue, that you would consider planning our wedding. After all, you found the venue and you know the local area. The wedding planner had months to find our dream venue and couldn't do it, but you came up with the perfect location right away."

Karla's insides quivered with possibility. Saskia and Ben's high-profile wedding would be a huge opportunity for so many Bellbrook businesses. The florist, the hotel, the local inn, restaurants, everyone would benefit from the over-the-top event. Not to mention Bellcroft itself. Over the past several months, Karla had sunk her entire net worth into renovating the dilapidated manor house. Her plan was to earn back the money by renting out the oceanside estate as a destination event venue. Saskia and Ben's wedding would be The Event of The Year. If they selected Bellcroft as the venue, Saskia's followers would line up to host events there. Bellcroft would become the new It Place.

Damian puffed away on his cigar. Plumes of smoke circled him like a smoky wreath.

"If you'd like, Ms. Bell, I can have your bag delivered to your cabin," the deckhand piped in after watching Karla shift her designer tote bag to avoid any cigar ash or tobacco smell from infiltrating it.

"It's kind of you to offer, but I'm not staying aboard overnight," Karla explained. "I don't need a cabin. I live nearby, and I have a dog—"

"But you already came aboard and checked in." The deckhand screwed up his face in confusion. "I delivered your luggage myself. You ordered a Cobb salad for lunch. I delivered it to your cabin. You thanked me from inside."

"That wasn't me." Karla shook her head. "You must be confusing me with another guest."

"We don't have any other guests," Damien interjected. "Are you sure you didn't come aboard earlier today, Karla?"

"Positive," Karla insisted.

"Then whose luggage did the deckhand deliver? Who ordered the Cobb salad for lunch?"

Karla shook her head and shrugged.

"It sounds like we have ourselves a mystery to solve," Damien blew out a trail of white smoke. "Where's Caitlin?"

TWO

A MYSTERIOUS STOWAWAY

CAITLIN APPEARED on deck as though she had been waiting for Damien to summon her. Karla gave the deckhand a quick sideways glance. Did he press a magic button under the bar that had summoned her, or did Caitlin have weirdly impeccable timing?

"It's possible we have an interloper on board," Damien informed his executive assistant. He urged the deckhand to fill her in about the luggage and Cobb salad he delivered to the mystery occupant in Karla's cabin.

"That's right," Caitlin agreed with the deckhand's version of events. "Karla's assistant boarded The Aquaholic this morning. She said she was dropping off luggage and prepping the cabin ahead of Karla's arrival." She opened her leather planner and flipped to a specific page. "She said her name was Jennifer."

"Jennifer?" Karla questioned. "I didn't send anyone. The only people who know I'm here are my sister, Max, and my mother, Lynn." Lynn also happened to be Karla's assistant, but she didn't mention that. Lynn couldn't have boarded The Aquaholic since she was at Shearlock Combs having her roots touched up, getting lowlights, and having her eyebrows shaped; a ritual that would have taken all morning. "I don't even know anyone named Jennifer."

"Did you speak with Jennifer?" Damien asked, enthralled by the mystery.

"Briefly," Caitlin admitted. "We rode to The Aquaholic together. She was waiting at the dock when the tender picked me up this morning. I had been ashore picking up a few things and exploring the town. The driver wasn't expecting her, so when she told me she was Karla's assistant, I gave permission for her to board."

"You should have called me," Karla interjected. "I would have given you a guided tour."

"That would have been lovely," Caitlin said. "From what I saw, Bellbrook is a beautiful, cozy little town, but my phone was ringing off the hook, and I was too distracted to really enjoy myself." She shrugged one shoulder. "So, I gave up and came back to my office." She went on to explain how she texted the crew member who had shuttled her to the shore, requesting that he pick her up. When she arrived at the dock to meet him, Karla's imposter assistant was already there with two large hot-pink, hard-side rolling suitcases she claimed belonged to Karla.

"I don't have pink luggage. My luggage is silver. And why would I bring two large suitcases for an overnight visit?" Karla added as further proof that she was not involved with the mystery woman's actions. "What did Jennifer look like?"

"Mid-twenties," Caitlin replied. "Trendy hair that's shaved on one side and long on the other. She was wearing a white tank top and a long, loose bohemian-style blue skirt. She had tattoos across the top of her chest and both shoulders. Lots of earrings and big, pink sunglasses. Oh, and she had a purse, a large brown leather satchel." She held her hands apart to illustrate the size of Jennifer's satchel. "It looked vintage, it had a nice patina."

"She doesn't sound familiar," Karla said, shaking her head.

Everyone else shook their heads and mumbled in agreement. They didn't recognize the description either.

"When we boarded The Aquaholic, I showed Jennifer to Karla's cabin," Caitlin continued. "I told her I would have the luggage delivered shortly. The next crew member I encountered was the deckhand. He delivered the luggage."

"I left it in the hall." The deckhand nodded in agreement. "I would've taken it inside, but when I knocked, she said to leave it outside the door. Then awhile later, she called the kitchen and ordered a Cobb salad. I delivered it. She thanked me from inside the room and told me to leave the tray outside." He looked at Karla. "I assumed, since it was your cabin, that you had ordered the salad."

"Well, someone ordered the damn salad," Damien concluded, rising to his feet and giving his cigar a puff. "And I'm sure as heck gonna find out who."

"Oooh, a mysterious stowaway," Saskia said, nudging her fiancé Ben in the ribs. "My followers will love this!" She futzed with the settings on her phone, leaned into him, held her phone at arm's length, tilted her head, puckered her lips, and took a selfie.

Following Damien's lead, they all stood up. Everyone except the deckhand followed Damien in a single-file line as he left the deck.

"Karla, wait!" Saskia grabbed Karla's hand. "A quick selfie for my followers?" she asked.

"Sure," Karla replied.

"Make a face like we're solving a mystery." Saskia formed a small *o* with her mouth, pressed her manicured index finger against her chin, and looked upwards and to the right as though she were performing mental gymnastics.

Playing along, Karla laid her hands on her cheeks and made her best *Home Alone* face.

Saskia snapped the pic, then they hurried to catch up with Damien, Ben, and Caitlin.

THEY GATHERED in huddled silence around the cabin door.

Damien knocked.

No answer.

He knocked again, louder this time.

The group collectively held their breath and cocked their ears toward the door, listening for sounds of life on the other side. Nothing.

"Maybe Jennifer already left," Saskia whispered.

"Every time the tender leaves or returns to The Aquaholic, the trip is logged and so are the passengers. The only tender that has left the yacht since Jennifer and I boarded is the boat that picked up Karla from shore," Caitlin said.

All eyes turned to Karla.

"No one got off the boat when it arrived to pick me up, and I was the only person aboard for the ride back," she informed them. "Well, me and Captain Peterson."

Damien cleared his throat. He knocked again and shouted, "Hello! Anyone there?"

Silence.

Ben squeezed the door handle and gave it a gentle push. "Locked," he said.

"Caitlin, find a key," Damien instructed.

"Already on it," she replied, tapping her phone screen.

Moments later, Captain Peterson rounded the corner toward them.

"I texted the steward, not you," Caitlin protested.

"He's busy meeting with the chef," Captain Peterson replied. "I thought it best not to keep you waiting."

"Thank you, Peterson," Damien said.

The small crowd parted to make room in the narrow hallway for the captain.

He unlocked the door and stepped back.

Damien squeezed the handle and cracked open the door just enough to poke his head inside. "Hello?"

Karla strained and stretched her neck, but the door wasn't open enough for her to get a glimpse inside the cabin.

Saskia squeezed herself between the door and her father. "Jennifer? Are you in there, Jennifer?"

Silence.

Damien opened the door the rest of the way and stepped inside. He strode to the other side of the cabin.

Saskia and Ben followed him.

Caitlin gestured for Karla to go ahead of her. Captain Peterson stayed just outside the door.

The room was dark; the curtains were drawn, and the lights were off.

Damien threw open the heavy white curtains, and sunlight flooded the room.

The cabin was larger and more luxurious than Karla had expected. She ignored the momentary pang of regret that she'd declined Damien's offer to spend the night. Aside from the dark wood floors, everything was white. White walls, furniture, linens, and accessories. There was even a white vase of white roses on the small round table in front of the window.

There was no doubt someone had been there. A half-eaten Cobb salad sat abandoned on the writing desk across from the bed. The bed was made, but the white linens were creased and rumpled as though someone had been lying there. The decorative pillows had been disturbed.

One large bright-pink, hard-side rolling suitcase lay, unopened, on the luggage rack beside the dresser. A pair of flip flops were neatly stowed underneath.

"Where is she?" Saskia asked no one in particular.

Ben checked the small closet. "Empty," he said.

Caitlin set her planner on the nightstand and pocketed her phone, then lowered herself to her hands and knees to look under the bed. "Nothing under here."

Captain Peterson stood in the doorway with his feet hip width apart and his arms crossed in front of his chest, as though poised to stop the intruder should she suddenly pop out and make a run for it.

Damien opened the sliding door and stepped out onto the narrow balcony, peering over the railing.

What if she went overboard? Karla kept the thought to herself, not wanting to jump to hasty conclusions or panic her clients with worst-case scenarios.

Karla found herself butted up against a door. She opened it and slipped into the ensuite washroom. It was small and efficient but still well-appointed and elegant. The room was narrow, spanning the same width as the deep soaker tub under the window on the far wall. Light streamed through the window. A puddle of water next to the tub caught Karla's eye when the sunlight reflected off it. Karla inched closer to the deep tub. It was full of water, almost to the top. Something floated there, just below the surface.

Karla's heart thumped hard. Her throat dried up, and she forced a swallow. Every cell in her body warned her not to look inside the tub. She ignored her body's warnings and took cautious, slow steps toward the tub.

"Caitlin, Peterson!" Damien's muffled voice came from the next room. "We need to organize a search. There's an unknown woman wandering around the ship."

"I don't think she's wandering," Karla called from the edge of the tub where she watched the woman's arms floating on the surface of the water with her body just below. Her voluminous blue skirt billowed on the surface and her dark hair drifted, obscuring her face. Her leafy tattoos were varying shades of green.

Damien appeared a few feet behind her. Karla

moved aside to give him an unobstructed view of the tub.

"Is that—?"

Karla nodded.

"Is she?"

Karla nodded again. "She's dead."

THREE

KARLA BELL-DIXON

"YOU DID GOOD, LA-LA," Dean praised his eldest daughter. "You prevented the witnesses from further contaminating the crime scene, and you separated everyone until we could question them individually." He winked. "You'd make a great cop."

"Thanks, Dad," Karla said. "I'm still shocked they listened to me. Damien Casey has never struck me as someone who obeys orders."

"You did exactly what Max'n'cheese and I would have done," Dean added, beaming with pride.

"Please don't call me that at work." Max paused long enough from photographing the inside of Jennifer's cabin to roll her eyes at Dean.

"Sorry, Officer Sheridan," Dean replied, calling his youngest daughter by her professional name.

Police Chief Dean Sheridan was Karla and Max's father. Although he was a consummate professional, when it came to his daughters, he sometimes blurred the boundary between his professional and personal life. This was understandable, considering his youngest daughter Max was an officer under his command.

Karla didn't mind Dean calling her La-la. He had called her that as long as she could remember. It had gone from annoying and slightly embarrassing when she was young, to comforting and familiar now that she was older. Max was eleven years younger than Karla; a fact that Karla sometimes forgot because Max had always seemed so much more mature and responsible than other people her age. She knew Max would reach the same milestone eventually and grow to embrace— or at least tolerate—her Dean-bestowed nickname, Max'n'cheese.

"I'll take your statement first, La-la." Dean opened his notebook to a blank page and clicked the top of his ball-point pen. "That way, you can observe the rest of the witness interviews and act as a liaison for us. If you happen to have any insight into whether everyone is telling us the truth, that would be very helpful and appreciated." He scrawled the date across the top of the empty page. The notebook and pen appeared doll-house-sized in Dean's massive hands.

"I only know Damien's Tell," Karla told her father. "I haven't spent enough time with the other witnesses to know their Tells yet."

"What's Damien's Tell?" Dean asked, pen poised to write.

"He narrows his eyes and turns his head ever so slightly to the side while making intense eye contact with the person he's lying to." Karla demonstrated the Tell as she spoke.

A Tell is a subconscious, involuntary action that people do when they lie. They don't realize they're doing it. It's usually subtle and sometimes lasts only a microsecond. It's the body's way of releasing the guilt and discomfort that accompanies a lie.

Since she was a little girl, Karla had been able to identify and isolate patterns in people's behaviour and recognize their individual Tells. Her personal motto was never to trust anyone until she figured out their Tell. But that wasn't always easy because not everyone had a Tell. Some people, like sociopaths for example, don't feel guilt or shame when they lie and therefore don't need a Tell. Some people have multiple Tells. They might have one for small white lies and another for bigger lies. Or they might have specific Tells for specific people. Some people are brutally honest and don't need Tells.

"But you might figure out Tells for the other witnesses, right?" Dean asked.

"If I spend enough time with them," Karla replied.

"Tell me what happened La-la."

Karla told Dean everything that happened from the moment she stepped onto the yacht tender until he and Max came aboard The Aquaholic from their police boat.

"Does Jennifer have a surname?" Dean asked when Karla had finished recounting her story.

Karla shrugged in reply. "Caitlin Lopez might know. She's the one who told us Jennifer's first name."

"Is Caitlin the witness who spoke with the deceased?"

Karla nodded.

Dean scanned the cabin and sighed. "Well, we'll start with her fingerprints," he said. "If Jennifer is in our system, we'll find her full name, and from there we can contact her next of kin to notify them."

"And you'll be able to figure out why she was here and why she pretended to be my assistant," Karla added.

"There's literally nothing in this cabin that points to Jennifer's identity," Max said, having switched from photographing the cabin to searching it with purple-gloved hands. "Where's her wallet?" she asked, rifling through the contents of the suitcase on the luggage rack.

"Her wallet could be inside the leather satchel she was carrying," Karla recalled. "Caitlin said she specifically noticed it because it looked vintage and had a nice patina."

"Well, it's not here now." Max tossed her purple latex hands in frustration.

"Neither is the second suitcase," Karla remarked, scanning the room for the missing luggage.

"Are you sure there's supposed to be two suitcases, La-la?" Dean asked.

"Both Caitlin and the deckhand who delivered the luggage to the cabin said Jennifer boarded the yacht with two bright-pink hard-side suitcases," Karla replied. "She told Caitlin they belonged to me. I remember commenting that I would never bring two large suitcases for an overnight visit. I'm an efficient packer."

She had to be. Karla's concierge job often had her jetting across the planet to fulfill some urgent request or other from her demanding clients.

"She must have more luggage," Max concurred, removing each item from the suitcase to photograph it. "This one is full of clothes, but no outfits. Only tops. Tank tops, t-shirts, a sweater, a hoodie, a denim jacket, and a bunch of slinky lingerie, but no practical underwear." She turned to face her sister and father. "So, unless Jennifer was planning to wear the same blue boho skirt and flip-flops but change her top and only wear slinky, lacy foundation garments that offer zero support, something's missing."

"Also, there are no toiletries in the washroom," Karla pointed out. "Her deodorant and such must be in the other suitcase with the rest of her clothes."

"Well, if two suitcases and a brown leather satchel came on board, they must be here somewhere," Dean theorized.

"Unless..." Max raised her eyebrows and shifted her gaze to the balcony door.

"I had the same thought," Karla confessed. "I worried Jennifer had gone overboard when we first entered the cabin and couldn't find her."

"It's *possible* the rest of Jennifer's luggage went overboard," Dean added, "but I don't think it's likely."

"Why not?" Max asked.

"Because this cabin faces shore. It's a beautiful summer day. The waterfront is full of locals and tourists enjoying the weather. Droves of people have visited the waterfront to see The Aquaholic since it arrived yesterday. It's not every day a state-of-the-art mega yacht drops anchor so close to our waterfront park. It's kind of become a tourist attraction. People are taking photos of it. Also, hard-side luggage floats before it sinks. Even if no one saw it fall, someone could have easily seen it floating around."

"So, if someone had tossed Jennifer's other suitcase off the balcony, there's a good chance someone would have seen it," Karla surmised.

"If the luggage is still on this ship, we'll find it," Dean said with confidence. "My officers are searching every square inch of this yacht."

"Assuming the killer got rid of the luggage, they wouldn't have thrown it overboard because they wouldn't have wanted to draw attention to it until they made their escape," Max added.

"Killer?" Karla asked. "You think Jennifer was

murdered?" She screwed up her face in confusion. "But the door was locked. If Jennifer was murdered, and the killer locked the door when they left, that means the killer had a key to the cabin."

"It might not be murder," Max reminded her. "But if Jennifer did this intentionally, she didn't leave a note." Max shrugged. "It could have been an accident or a medical episode." She let out an exasperated sigh. "When we discover the deceased's identity, we'll be able to find out if she had any underlying health issues that might explain her sudden death."

It wouldn't explain her missing belongings though, Karla thought to herself.

"We can't say for sure yet that it was murder, La-la," Dean said. "But every death scene is a crime scene until the coroner confirms the cause of death."

Karla picked up on Dean's *yet*. Reading between the lines, she knew Dean suspected Jennifer's death was murder, but he was waiting for the coroner to confirm it.

"Speaking of the coroner, where is Rob?" Karla checked the time on her phone and noticed seventeen text message notifications from Lynn. *I'll have to deal with those later,* she thought, locking the screen.

"She'll be here any minute," Dean replied. "The yacht tender is picking her up from shore as we speak."

"Damien Casey is being as cooperative as possible," Max said. "He offered us exclusive use of his yacht tender and driver. So, we have that and our police boat at our disposal." Max eyed something on the floor suspiciously. "What's this?" She crouched down. "There's something half hidden under the bed." She popped up again, clutching Caitlin Lopez's dark leather planner in her purple-gloved hand.

"That's Caitlin's planner," Karla said. "She must have dropped it in all the confusion when we discovered Jennifer's body."

"I almost missed it," Max said. "It was camouflaged against the dark wood floor."

"Caitlin must be freaking out looking for it," Karla added. "I'd be frantic if I misplaced my planner. It's like an extension of my brain. It's more reliable than my memory."

"Are you sure it belongs to Caitlin, La-la?"

"One hundred percent."

"Are you sure Caitlin brought it with her into the room?" Dean asked.

"Is there any chance it was already in the room when you guys arrived?" Max clarified.

Karla thought back to the events on the deck before they came to the cabin. "It was with her when we entered the cabin. I remember her opening it on the deck earlier to search for Jennifer's name."

Max popped the clasp on the planner and opened the cover. "Let's see if she wrote anything else about Jennifer, shall we?"

Karla repositioned herself beside Max, so she could look at the planner pages for herself.

The first page had Caitlin's name, contact information, and a note offering a reward for the planner's return should someone find it.

Max flipped through the calendar pages which were covered in notes and annotations, some highlighted and some crossed out, underlined, or circled. It was beautifully chaotic, not unlike Karla's own planner. An archive of a busy life. She flipped to the notes section at the back of the planner. The first page was covered in doodles. Mostly Caitlin practicing her signature as *Caitlin Casey* in fancy handwriting, sometimes with hearts drawn around the pretend signatures.

"This reminds me of when you were in high school, and I opened your notebook and found out you had been practicing your signature with Griff's last name," Max teased with an impish grin. "Mrs. Griffin Dixon." She pinched her thumb and index finger together and pretended to write in the air. "Karla Bell-Dixon."

The streak was over. It had been two weeks since anyone had mentioned Griff's name to Karla. Two blissful, peaceful weeks. With Griff out of town on a family vacation until the end of the month, and with the renovation work on the manor house at least ninety-percent complete, Karla had, for the first time since returning to Bellbrook, managed to put her handsome, charming, and funny former high school sweetheart, Griff Dixon, out of her mind. Until now. *Thanks a lot, Max.*

"Shut up, Max'n'cheese!" Karla shoved Max with her hip.

"Hey, don't call me that at work." Max returned her sister's hip check.

"Girls." Dean's voice was deep and authoritative. "Focus." His phone chimed, and he checked the screen. "Rob's here," he said. "She just boarded the yacht."

"Are Damien Casey and Caitlin an item?" Max asked, looking at a two-page spread of Caitlin's doodles and variations of her signature as Caitlin Casey.

"Not that I'm aware of," Karla replied. "Caitlin has been Damien's executive assistant for about twenty years. They live on the yacht together much of the year."

"Most assistants don't live with their employer," Dean pointed out.

"Max, why don't you return Caitlin's planner and take her statement."

Max nodded.

"La-la, go with her as our liaison and let us know if you believe Ms. Lopez's version of events."

FOUR

CLARK

"THANK GOODNESS!" Caitlin exclaimed when she opened her cabin door to find Max and Karla standing there. "I think I left my planner in the other—"

Max held up the planner. Caitlin stopped talking mid-sentence. Her shoulders dropped, and she let out a sigh of obvious relief.

"It was on the floor next to the bed," Max said.

"I put it on the nightstand," Caitlin explained. "It must have fallen in all the confusion. It was quite crowded in there with all of us."

"I'd like to ask you some questions about what happened," Max said, handing Caitlin her prized possession.

"Come in." Caitlin stood aside so Karla and Max could step inside her cabin.

Karla placed her sun hat on the small table just

inside the door and set her tote bag on the floor next to it.

Max's phone chimed. She checked the screen, then pocketed her phone, ignoring the notification.

Caitlin's cabin was identical in layout to the cabin where they had found Jennifer's lifeless body. Except Caitlin's cabin was on the other side of the ship with a beautiful, endless ocean view, and was more personalized than the elegant white cabin Karla and Max had just left. Family photos dotted Caitlin's walls and dressers. Her floral bedding and personal items strewn about the space made it feel homier and less formal than the elegant all-white cabin where Jennifer died.

"Did you look inside my planner?" Caitlin asked. "There's sensitive, confidential information in there." She opened the book and flipped through it, as if to satisfy herself that the contents were still intact. "I know I shouldn't keep sensitive information in here, but sometimes I just jot things down in a hurry before I forget. I'm not always near a computer." She looked at Karla. "You know how it is."

"Yes, I do." Karla smiled.

"I leafed through your planner when I found it," Max admitted. "At first, I thought it might have belonged to the deceased."

"Right." Caitlin nodded. "Have you found out who she is, and why she was here?"

"Not yet," Max replied. "I was hoping you might

know more about her. It seems you were the only person who spoke with her face to face."

"Only for a moment," Caitlin clarified. "She was waiting at the dock when I arrived to meet the tender. She introduced herself as Jennifer and told me she was Karla's assistant. The way she said it sounded like I should have been expecting her. She said Karla had sent her to drop off luggage and prepare the cabin for Karla's arrival." Caitlin shrugged. "I had no reason not to believe her."

Max's phone chimed again. She checked the screen, shot the device an annoyed look, and switched off the sound so it would only vibrate instead of ring and chime.

"Tell me everything, starting with the moment you saw her on the dock," Max instructed, her pen and notebook poised for action.

Caitlin told Max the same story she had told earlier on the deck. She mentioned Jennifer's two pieces of luggage and a large brown leather purse. She described Jennifer's hair, sunglasses, earrings, and tattoos. Caitlin recalled with detail the outfit Jennifer wore; the same outfit she was wearing when they discovered her body floating in the bathtub.

"That's it?" Max confirmed at the end of Caitlin's story.

Caitlin shrugged. "I wish I knew more."

"Where did you go after you escorted Jennifer to her cabin?" Max asked.

"I was working until Karla arrived," Caitlin replied. "Damien and I are *very* busy right now. He has several projects on the go."

"So, you were in your office?" Max asked.

Caitlin nodded.

Karla was trying to focus on Caitlin, to determine her Tell, but got distracted every few minutes by Max's vibrating cell phone.

"Do you live aboard The Aquaholic year-round?" Max asked.

"Pretty much," Caitlin confirmed. "I go where Damien goes, and he spends six to nine months of the year aboard his yacht."

"Floating around the world must complicate your personal life," Karla suggested, hoping to create a smooth segue into discussing Caitlin's relationship status.

"How do you mean?" Caitlin asked.

"I mean, it must be difficult to maintain relationships when you're always moving around and far away from land."

"I'm married to my career," Caitlin said. "Damien is very generous with giving me time off and *very* accommodating when I want to spend time with my family." She gestured to the family photos that adorned her desk. "He's a *very* generous employer. I make a point of flying out to visit my sister and her family at least every other month. And sometimes, Damien flies them here for a vacation. My niece and nephew love The Aquaholic, and they adore Damien. He often makes time to take them fishing or tubing so I can spend quality time with my sister. We're only a year apart, and we're very close."

"Karla and I are very close too," Max said, "even though we're eleven years apart."

"Oh." Caitlin looked back and forth from Max to Karla quizzically. "You two are sisters? I never would have guessed."

"Same dad, different moms," Karla explained.

Caitlin nodded as though this made sense.

No one ever guessed that Karla and Max were sisters. On the surface, Dean's genes were nowhere to be found. Aside from sharing the same 5'5 height and foot size, Karla and Max looked like they were born on opposite sides of the world. Both women were near clones of their mothers. Max's brown eyes and dark straight hair were the opposite of Karla's green eyes and blonde wavy hair. They even inherited their mothers' mannerisms. And Max was bilingual thanks to spending every summer of her childhood in her mother's hometown in Japan.

"OK, but other than your sister," Karla said. "How do you maintain *other* personal relationships when you move around so much?"

"Other personal relationships?" Caitlin's confused squint made it clear that she didn't understand what Karla was alluding to.

"Are you and Damien..." Max's voice trailed off

before she finished her question, but the insinuation was clear. She was asking if Caitlin and Damien had a romantic relationship.

"No." Caitlin was emphatic. "Our relationship is strictly professional. Damien would *never* date an employee. He knows better. Scandals like that destroy careers like his." She let out a small huff. "Besides, I'm not his type," she added under her breath.

"Damien has a type?" Max asked.

"Maybe," Caitlin shrugged one shoulder. "I dunno."

"You've known Damien for almost two decades," Karla challenged. "You spend more time with him than anyone else, including his daughter. You know everything about him. I'm sure you've noticed what type of woman Damien Casey finds attractive."

"He keeps his personal relationships low profile," Caitlin admitted. "When Damien is dating someone, it's practically a secret. He doesn't like the people he works with to know too much about his personal life. Except for me, of course. He tells me." She looked around as though she was making sure there was no one else in the cabin, eavesdropping on their conversation. "He doesn't even introduce his lady friends to Saskia unless it's really serious."

"Was Jennifer his type?" Max asked.

"Are you suggesting Jennifer came aboard The Aquaholic because Damien invited her?" Caitlin demanded, her volume increasing with each word. "That she was here for a secret rendezvous with him?"

"No," Karla replied, hoping to deescalate the offense Caitlin displayed on her employer's behalf. "We need to investigate every possible reason Jennifer could have snuck aboard, no matter how unlikely."

"Maybe you sent her," Caitlin accused, pointing at Karla. "After all, she said she was *your* assistant. How did she know your name? How did she know you were going to be here today? How did she know Damien had prepared a cabin for you?"

"I didn't send her," Karla said. "I've never seen her before. Whoever Jennifer is, she's not from Bellbrook, and she doesn't work for Just Task Me!"

"Well, she's not Damien's type," Caitlin defended. "First, she's too young. Damien prefers women his own age. Second, I've never known him to date someone so... so... trendy. The earrings, the tattoos, the half-shaved head, they aren't Damien's style. He prefers classy, professional, politically connected women who he can have intellectually stimulating conversations with."

Could Jennifer have been politically connected?

"If Damien and Jennifer were friends, I would know about it. Part of my job is protecting Damien's privacy and keeping his name out of the tabloids. I facilitate his dates, meetings, getaways, and even smooth over his break ups."

"Can you think of any reason Jennifer might have snuck aboard?" Max asked. "Even if you think it's far-fetched, I'd still like to hear it."

Caitlin shrugged one shoulder and shook her head in a way that made Karla wonder if she was having an internal debate about whether to say something out loud. "It's possible that maybe Jennifer was a jersey chaser?" Her voice was barely a whisper.

"A what?" Max asked, her pen hovering over the notebook page.

"A jersey chaser," Caitlin repeated. "It's a crude name for football groupies."

"You think Jennifer might have snuck aboard for Ben?" Karla asked.

"It's possible," Caitlin replied. "He was a professional football player, and now he's famous because of his relationship with Saskia." She let out a soft chuckle and snort. "Saskia puts their entire relationship on social media. Ben is a good-looking guy. We've had previous issues with women going to extreme lengths trying to get near him."

"Thanks," Max said. "We'll look into it."

Sensing that they had overstayed their welcome, Max thanked Caitlin for her statement and for helping with their inquiries.

Karla hoisted her tote bag over her shoulder as Caitlin thanked them for returning her planner.

"You didn't ask her about the doodles," Karla whispered to Max after they left Caitlin's cabin.

"Caitlin's feelings for Damien are only relevant if Jennifer was murdered," Max reasoned. "It's likely Jennifer's death was an accident or something. And I didn't want to upset her. You saw how defensive she got when we asked if she and Damien were a couple. If I'd mentioned the doodles, she probably would have shut down the conversation and thrown us out of her cabin."

"I noticed how defensive she was too," Karla said. "She's quite protective of him."

Could Caitlin Lopez be protective enough of Damien Casey to kill for him?

"WHAT'S GOING ON?" Max asked. "Why are you guys out in the hall instead of inside the cabin?"

"Clark is in there," Dean replied, jerking his head toward the cabin door.

"We're staying out of his way while he does his thing," Rob elaborated. "He's finishing his search of the ship."

K-9 Constable Clark was Bellbrook PD's police dog. He was a three-year-old Belgian Malinois and local celebrity, often making appearances at community events, and local schools.

"We haven't found the missing luggage yet, but if it's on this ship, Clark will find it," Dean said with certainty.

Max and Dean wandered down the hall while she debriefed him about her and Karla's conversation with Caitlin.

"Do you have any SPF in there?" Rob asked, nodding at Karla's tote bag. "I was expecting to work inside today, not in the middle of the ocean on a sunny day."

"I've got your back, my fair-skinned friend." Karla rummaged through her bag for the travel size bottle of sunscreen she remembered putting in there this morning. "Keep it," she said, handing her best friend the small tube. "I have plenty, and you need it more than me."

Karla used sunscreen for its anti-wrinkle, anti-aging benefits, not because she was prone to burn. In fact, Karla had never had a nasty sunburn. She was one of the lucky ones whose skin broke out in a sun-kissed glow. Rob, on the other hand, was an alabaster redhead with skin so sensitive it turned an angry shade of red within minutes of exposure to the sun's rays. Growing up, Karla had spent many summers rubbing SPF into her best friend's back at the beach. She sometimes felt guilty when her friend would suffer tender burns and her skin would peel, while Karla's biggest sun-related inconvenience was an occasional tan line under her jewellery.

"What do you think about Jennifer?" Karla asked as Rob slathered sunscreen on the back of her neck and the exposed parts of her arms, protecting her clusters of red freckles from the harmful UV rays.

"It's a head scratcher," Rob admitted, adjusting her long ginger ponytail so it wouldn't stick to her lotioned neck. "It could be a medical episode. I'll know more once she's on my exam table. I don't observe any obvious signs of foul play or trauma. Dean said there are items missing from the room, and they can't find anything to identify her, so even if her death isn't suspicious, the circumstances surrounding it are."

Karla nodded and, before she could ask Rob if, in her professional opinion, Jennifer could have been murdered, the cabin door opened.

"All clear, Dr. Mayhew," said Clark's handler.

"Thanks," Rob smiled. "May we pet Clark?"

Dr. Robyn Mayhew was Bellbrook's resident family doctor and moonlighted as the town coroner on an as-needed basis. Like Karla, she immediately loved every dog, cat, and other domesticated animal she met.

"Sure," replied the handler.

Rob and Karla took turns scratching Clark between the ears and telling him he was a good boy. The large dog lapped up the attention, panting happily and thrashing his tail with glee.

Karla's phone vibrated inside her purse. She stopped petting Clark to check it. Twenty-seven messages from Lynn.

"Lynn's trying to reach you," Max called from down the hall. "She's texted me eleven times asking where you are."

"Something must be up," Karla said, furrowing her brow at the notifications on her phone. "I should get back to shore and find out what she wants." She looked at Dean. "Am I allowed to leave?"

Dean nodded. "I'll ask the tender driver to take you back to shore."

"Actually, I'm taking Clark back on the police boat if you need a lift," the handler offered.

Dean nodded his approval.

"That would be great," Karla replied. "Thank you."

FIVE

NOT JUST A PRETTY FACE

LYNN WAS PACING on the dock and checking her phone when the police boat arrived. Gucci, tethered to her by his Fendi leash and collar, obediently paced alongside.

Karla stepped onto the wooden dock and crouched to greet her petite pup. To her dismay, but not her surprise, Gucci charged right past her and straight toward Clark. The adorably dishevelled small terrier sniffed Clark's enormous paws and jumped to sniff his alert ears while Karla thanked Clark's handler for the ride.

"C'mon, Gooch!" Karla took the leash from Lynn and gently tugged Gucci away from the patient object of his attention. "Let's go," she urged.

"Thank you for taking care of Gucci," Karla said to her mother as they made their way toward the parking lot.

"According to your schedule, you should only have been aboard The Aquaholic for an hour. Then you were supposed to give Saskia and Ben a tour of Bellcroft."

"We had to postpone the tour until tomorrow," Karla said.

"Lucky for you, we're supposed to have this amazing weather all week," Lynn said, gesturing to the blue, sunny sky. "It would be a shame if Saskia and Ben had to tour Bellcroft in the rain." She stopped walking, pressed one nostril closed and inhaled deeply, then pressed the other nostril closed and inhaled again. "Crystal clear," she declared. "No rain for at least four days.

"That's a relief." Karla was grateful for her sunglasses because they hid her eye roll.

Lynn believed her body had barometric superpowers. She swore her sinuses could predict rain, and her left hip could predict snow. As far as Karla knew, Lynn's sinuses and hip had never been wrong, but she still didn't like to encourage her mother's meteorological quirk.

"You've been aboard the yacht all afternoon. If we don't hurry, we'll be late for dinner at Rosalie's house."

"I forgot about dinner at Rosalie's," Karla said, suddenly aware of the hollow rumble in her tummy. "With all the excitement, I missed lunch."

"Why?" Lynn asked. "What happened? Everyone in town is saying police officers and Rob have been going back and forth between the shore and the yacht."

"All I can say is someone snuck aboard, and some luggage is missing."

"That doesn't explain why Rob is there," Lynn pressed. "Is she there as a doctor or a coroner? Did someone get sick?" She studied Karla's face for a hint of reaction. Nothing. "Did someone die?"

"I'm not at liberty to say anything," Karla replied.

"But—" Lynn continued.

"Why did you send me a gazillion texts?" Karla asked, interrupting her mother and changing the subject. "You know I turn off my phone when I'm with a client. Max said you texted her a dozen times when you couldn't reach me."

"It was an emergency," Lynn insisted. "Just Task Me's website crashed from too much traffic. The phone line at your main office went down because it was overwhelmed with incoming calls, and you've gained over ten thousand new social media followers in the past three hours. It was crazy."

Karla stopped dead in her tracks. Gucci kept walking until he ran out of leash, then turned to see what was holding them up.

"Were we hacked? What happened?" Worst-case scenarios swirled through Karla's brain.

"Saskia Casey happened," Lynn replied. "She posted a selfie of you and her. It went viral and blew up the website, phone line, and Just Task Me's social media accounts." She made a mock explosion with her hands, complete with sound effects.

Lynn had a knack for hyperbole, so Karla checked for herself in case Lynn was exaggerating.

"Haven't you seen it?"

"No, I haven't." Karla pulled out her phone and unlocked the screen. She scrolled through the dozens of notifications from Lynn and stopped on a notification from the car dealership. "Shoot! My car isn't ready. They're still waiting for the part to arrive. It won't be ready until tomorrow at the earliest."

"Don't worry, love," Lynn reassured her. "I'll drive you wherever you need to go until you get your car back."

"Thanks, Mother." Karla hated to be a burden; relying on other people went against her fiercely independent nature.

She opened the social media apps on her phone and searched for Saskia's profile.

There it was. The photo Saskia took of her and Karla on the upper deck of The Aquaholic. Saskia's contemplative face and Karla's shocked expression with the caption, *Off to solve a mystery with the world's best wedding planner. The case of the mysterious stowaway.* Followed by six mystery and wedding related emojis. Saskia tagged Just Task Me's social media account. Karla checked Just Task Me's social media page. Twelve thousand new followers today so far. And hundreds if not thousands of comments on her most recent posts.

"Wow," Karla said. "I knew Saskia had a powerful

social media presence, but I didn't realize how dedicated her followers are."

"They're beyond dedicated. They're rabid," Lynn corrected. "Did you know they call themselves Saskians? They have groups and websites devoted to obsessing over her and copying her style. Since she posted that photo of you and her, Saskians all over the world want to hire you to plan their next big event or get details about Saskia and Ben's upcoming nuptials."

"She hasn't even approved the venue yet," Karla said. "Imagine how busy we'll be after the wedding when she posts photos and videos from the big day."

They arrived at Lynn's car, and she unlocked the doors using the remote on her keychain.

"I'll have to miss dinner," Karla lamented as she positioned herself in the passenger seat with Gucci on her lap.

"You can't miss dinner," Lynn argued. "Rosalie will be devastated. She went to a lot of trouble. You know how much she looks forward to feeding us. You have to come."

"Mother, my website and phone lines crashed. That has to be my priority."

Lynn took her hand off the gearshift and flicked her wrist dismissively. "I took care of the website and the phone lines," she said. "And I've reposted Saskia's social media post on Just Task Me's account. I've already started sorting through the hundreds of comments in case any of them are actual, good leads for new clients."

"Seriously?" Karla didn't even try to hide the shock in her voice. "How did you know what to do?"

"A good assistant is resourceful and always figures out what to do." Lynn shifted the car into reverse and eased it out of the parking spot. "I contacted your IT guy about the website. He worked his magic, and the website is back. He's monitoring it, so hopefully it won't crash again. I called your office manager at the head office about the land line. She called the phone company. They fixed it within a couple of hours."

"Wow. Thank you, Mother." Karla let out a relieved sigh. "Hiring you might be one of the best things I've ever done."

"I told you I'd be a brilliant assistant." Lynn grinned and used her *I told you so* voice. "I'm not just a pretty face, you know." She gave her daughter a sly side-eye and playful wink. "You didn't just inherit your looks from me. You inherited your brain, too."

Karla couldn't deny the resemblance. They had the same wavy blonde hair, but Lynn's was longer than Karla's shoulder-length bob. Their facial features were nearly identical, except Karla had green eyes, a combination of Lynn's blue eyes and Dean's hazel eyes.

"I inherited some of Dad's qualities too," Karla added in Dean's defence.

"You inherited his strong moral compass and his

empathetic nature," Lynn agreed. "I'm just relieved you didn't inherit his flattop haircut."

Karla bit her lip but laughed despite herself.

GUCCI RAN into the house and disappeared down the hall, no doubt in search of his favourite feline friend, Purrnest Hemingway, lovingly called, Hemi.

Rosalie Howard's house was always the perfect temperature and always smelled like home cooking and unconditional love. The lady herself always smelled like Ponds cold cream and total acceptance. Her antiques-crowded house struck the perfect balance between cozy and welcoming.

Karla went into the kitchen and rearranged the jam-packed fridge to make space for the wine she and Lynn had brought for dinner.

"Grab a knife and slice these cucumbers." Rosalie placed a cucumber and cutting board on the kitchen table, next to where she was pitting an avocado.

"Yes, ma'am," Karla replied, doing as she was told.

"Lynn, you're on red onion duty," Rosalie advised. "Thinly sliced, please."

"Whatever you say, Rosalie," Lynn said, joining them at the kitchen table.

The three women chatted, chopped, sliced, and laughed while they assembled the heirloom tomato salad with couscous that would be their side dish.

"It's a beautiful evening," Rosalie observed. "I thought we could eat alfresco."

"That sounds wonderful," Lynn agreed. "I can't think of a better view than your beautiful garden, Rosalie. We should take advantage of the long days and warm evenings while they last."

Whining and meowing at the back door interrupted their relaxed conversation.

"Gucci and Hemi want to go outside," Rosalie announced, pushing her chair away from the table.

"I'll go," Lynn insisted, standing up first. "You stay here."

"It's fine. I need to take the chicken off the rotisserie anyway," Rosalie argued, pointing toward the backyard where her gas barbecue lived.

"I think I can carry a chicken from the backyard to the kitchen," Lynn said.

Rosalie shot her a dubious look that suggested otherwise.

"Fine," the octogenarian reluctantly relented. "There's a serving plate on the table by the back door."

Lynn washed the onion residue off her hands and headed toward the backdoor, assuring Gucci and Hemi that their release into the backyard was imminent.

"It's nice to see you and Lynn getting along so well," Rosalie commented as she shook up the mason jar of lemon juice, olive oil, and fresh chopped cilantro that would dress their salad.

"We've come a long way," Karla admitted with a

sigh. "Our relationship is far from perfect, but we've grown closer in the past nine months than the rest of the forty years I've been alive."

"May would be thrilled," Rosalie said with a wide smile. "There's nothing she wanted more in the world than for you and Lynn, the two people she loved most, to take care of each other after she left." She squeezed Karla's hand and wistfulness twinkled in her brown eyes.

Grandma May didn't leave. She died. But Rosalie always used a euphemism that sounded less harsh than death. They were best friends. Grandma May and Rosalie saw each other almost every day of their lives for over sixty years. If they couldn't see each other in person, they spoke on the phone. They spent so much time at each other's houses that they wore a path in the ground between their back doors. The path that Karla ensured was left untouched when she renovated Grandma May's cottage. The path that she walked with Gucci every day. Rosalie and Grandma May were so close that until she was six, Karla thought Rosalie was her grandmother too. She was not, but only in the biological sense of the word. Rosalie, Lynn, and Karla had helped each other through their matriarch's death last fall, clinging to each other while they learned how to live with the Grandma May-shaped holes in their hearts.

"I still catch myself unlocking my back door every morning so May won't have to knock," Rosalie said, smiling sadly and gazing in the general direction of nostalgia.

"Chicken's here!" Lynn crooned in a sing-song voice as she swept into the kitchen. "Three chickens might be a bit much for one meal, Rosalie."

"Nonsense," Rosalie said, rising to her feet. "I'm sending both of you home with leftovers for yourselves, Max, Dean, and Rob. I hear they've had a hectic day on the water. They'll need a hearty meal."

Does anything happen in this town that Rosalie doesn't know about? Karla wondered.

Feeding the people she loved was Rosalie's love language. Her overflowing fridge, freezers, and pantry were physical manifestations of her overflowing heart.

"Lynn, you set the table," Rosalie instructed. "Karla, you carry the chicken and the salad. I'll bring the wine and the bread."

Standing at the counter, carving and plating the slow-cooked rotisserie chicken seasoned with herbes de Provence, Rosalie Howard stood a hair under five feet tall in her purple rubber gardening clogs, light blue pants with an elasticized waistband, and purple t-shirt that said, *I love gardening from my head to my tomatoes.* Her earrings always matched her outfit. Today's earrings were daisy studs with purple petals and light-blue centres.

Despite her diminutive stature, Rosalie Howard was an unstoppable force in the Bellbrook community. Her opinion was widely sought after and highly regarded on many local matters. She was president of the local gardening club, and organized more community events than Karla could count. She didn't let her age—she was eighty years young—stop her from doing anything. Ever. Rosalie's dark skin was care-worn, and her once dark hair was more silver than not, but when she laughed and her dimples appeared, Karla could catch a glimpse of the young woman she once was.

DINNER WAS DELICIOUS. Birds singing in the trees accompanied their meal, and Gucci and Hemi lurked at their feet, hoping someone would drop scraps. Karla, Lynn, and Rosalie took turns pitying the persistent pets and snuck them bits of chicken under the table. The chicken was tender and moist, and the salad was seasonal perfection. The food fed their bodies, and the good company and conversation fed their souls.

"I think I'll have a bit more of everything," Lynn announced, reaching for the salad bowl. "It's so delicious."

"Save room for dessert," Rosalie warned. "I made blueberry squares."

"Mmm, blueberry squares are my favourite," Karla mumbled with a mouth full of salad.

"I'm glad to hear it," Rosalie responded. "I made an extra batch for each of you to take home."

Rosalie has spent more time cooking today than I have in my entire life, Karla mused to herself.

"I've been meaning to mention," Karla said, picking up her wine glass and touching Lynn's hair. "Your hair looks amazing. I mean, it's always perfect, but it seems a little extra perfect today."

"Thanks, love." Lynn smoothed her long blonde locks behind her ears and pushed her hair behind her shoulder. "Jennifer did a fabulous job."

Jennifer?!

SIX

JENNIFER-LEILA

"JENNIFER?" Karla asked, flabbergasted that this name had come up again. "I thought Ava was your hairdresser?"

"Ava's on maternity leave, love," Lynn explained. "She's due to have the twins any day now."

"Right, I forgot," Karla said.

"Jennifer is filling in for her. I was nervous, at first, about trusting someone new with my hair, but Ava trained her and highly recommended her." Lynn smoothed her tresses again. "I'm happy with the result."

"What does Jennifer look like?" Karla asked.

"Why?" Lynn asked, tilting her head and squeezing together her professionally shaped brows.

"Remember, I told you that someone snuck aboard The Aquaholic?"

Lynn nodded.

"I heard about that," Rosalie said. "Apparently some luggage went missing too."

"That's right," Karla confirmed. "Well, the intruder called herself Jennifer."

"Oh well, it couldn't be my Jennifer," Lynn theorized. "I was in her chair all morning and when I left, she said she had back-to-back appointments all afternoon." She gazed into the distance and swirled the last bit of wine in her glass. "I hope it's not the same Jennifer. I'd hate to lose another hairdresser."

"What does Jennifer look like, Lynn?" Rosalie refocussed Lynn on the topic at hand.

"She's quite young," Lynn replied. "Taller than me, but not by much. Long dark hair with highlights and long bangs that cover her eyebrows. She's chatty and friendly with a lot of energy."

"That doesn't match the description of the person who infiltrated The Aquaholic." Karla sighed. "I guess Jennifer is a pretty popular name."

"What did the other Jennifer look like?" Rosalie asked.

"Dark hair that's shaved on one side and long on the other," Karla recalled. "Lots of earrings, and"—she swept her hand across her chest from one shoulder to the other—"an intricate tattoo that stretches across her chest and throat from shoulder to shoulder."

"Vines?" Lynn asked. "Are her tattoos green vines that start on each shoulder, meet in the middle, and wrap around her neck like they're choking her?"

"Yes!" Karla slapped the table, amazed by the accuracy of Lynn's description. "You know her?"

"She sounds like the tourist I met at Shearlock Combs today," Lynn replied. "But her name wasn't Jennifer, it was Leila."

"Maybe Jennifer and Leila are the same person," Rosalie suggested. "If she trespassed onto someone's yacht, she might have lied about her name so she wouldn't get caught."

"For all I know, she lied when she told me her name was Leila," Lynn pointed out. "It's not like I checked her ID or anything."

"Did you speak to Leila?" Karla asked.

"Oh, yes!" Lynn replied. "We sat next to each other and had a nice long natter. I was waiting for my highlights to marinate, and she was getting a mani-pedi."

"What did you and Leila talk about?" Rosalie asked, pouring herself another glass of wine and settling into her chair, prepared to consume Lynn's response like the juicy gossip it was.

"This and that," Lynn replied. "She said she was in town for a few days to meet up with her boyfriend. Apparently, he travels for work, so they only get to see each other every few weeks. He flies her into whichever town he's in, and they spend time together before he leaves again."

"Did she tell you where she's staying?" Karla asked.

There is only one hotel in town, The Seascape, and one bed and breakfast, the Nestled Inn, but Jenniferslash-Leila could have stayed in one of the many vacation rentals that had popped up in Bellbrook over the past few years.

"She said she's got an ocean view room at the Seascape," Lynn replied. "She went on and on about how excited she was to see her boyfriend. She's completely smitten with him. She told us she brought so much lingerie on this trip that it filled almost an entire suitcase."

It sure did, Karla thought to herself, recalling the suitcase Max had searched that only contained tops and sexy lingerie.

"Did she mention her boyfriend's name or what he does for a living that brought him to Bellbrook?" Karla asked.

"She wouldn't tell Jennifer and me his name. She said he works in an environment with sensitive information and a lot of security, so they have to be discreet when they get together." Lynn drained her wine glass and placed it on the table. "She wanted to take him out to dinner tonight and asked us to recommend a restaurant with a romantic ambience and good food. Somewhere local so they could enjoy a bottle of champagne and not have to worry about driving back to the hotel."

"Where did you suggest?" Rosalie asked.

"La Truffe Noire," Lynn replied. "It's the nicest restaurant in town, and it's the most intimate. We told her to tell the maître'd that Lynn and Jennifer sent her and recommended table five." She looked at Karla. "It's the best one in the restaurant. Corner table with windows on two sides overlooking the ocean."

Comprehension fluttered in Karla's belly.

"Did you introduce yourself to Leila? Did you say, 'My name is Lynn?'"

"I don't think so," Lynn replied, shaking her head. "We started talking, and she said, 'My name is Leila.' Then Jennifer, who was putting in my foils, said 'We're Lynn and Jennifer, it's nice to meet you.'"

The flutter in Karla's belly grew bigger and spread to her chest.

"Did you tell her what you do for a living?"

"I might have mentioned it," Lynn admitted. "We were talking about The Aquaholic and how big and modern it is. Jennifer googled it and found out it's worth over ten million dollars. Then she said she'd love to see what it looked like on the inside." Lynn gazed sheepishly at her hands wringing in her lap. "And... I might have mentioned... that you're Damien Casey's private concierge, and I'm your assistant, and you were visiting the yacht to meet with your client and... He even offered you a cabin so you could stay the night, but you declined because you live close by and don't like to leave Gucci overnight if you don't have to."

Lynn's voice was so quiet and her words became so fast as she spoke, Karla could barely keep up with her confession.

"Mother, you know we never discuss clients with anyone who doesn't work for Just Task Me!" Karla admonished. "One reason Just Task Me! can attract VIP clients is because of our reputation for discretion."

"I know, love, and I'm sorry! It won't happen again, I swear." Lynn made an X across her heart with a French-manicured index finger. "They were so impressed by the yacht, and they caught me up in the moment…"

"Let's talk about this later," Karla said, pulling out her phone and texting Max and Dean.

"BECAUSE JENNIFER INTRODUCED herself and Lynn at the same time, Leila mixed them up. She thought the hairdresser's name was Lynn, and my mother's name was Jennifer. It was an honest mistake," Karla summarized, drying the glass food container that had held Dean's serving of chicken and salad.

Dean positioned his fork on the edge of his plate, knitted his brows together as he connected the mental dots, then said, "So you're suggesting the deceased's name isn't Jennifer, it's Leila, and she introduced herself as Jennifer because she mixed up Lynn and Jennifer when she met them together at Shearlock Combs. She thought Lynn was Jennifer, and Jennifer was Lynn, and therefore your assistant's name was Jennifer, not Lynn."

"Right." Karla nodded with enthusiasm as she snapped the lid onto the empty food container.

"It's plausible." Dean nodded and shovelled the last forkful of chicken into his mouth.

"This explains how she knew my name, that I had a meeting with Damien onboard the yacht, and why she claimed to be my assistant," Karla continued. "If I'm right, that's one mystery solved." She placed the clean, dry container on the table by her front door so she would remember to return it to Rosalie. "But we still don't know *why* she snuck onto the yacht."

"Whether her name is Jennifer or Leila—her finger-prints aren't on file," Dean revealed. "Her description doesn't match any missing person's reports for our department or the surrounding area. Max'n'cheese is at the station now widening the search." He washed down his meal with a tall glass of water, having declined Karla's offer of beer because he was working late on the mysterious woman's death.

"Caitlin and Lynn both said Leila didn't have a noticeable accent, and she mentioned nothing about where she lived," Karla agreed, clearing Dean's plate and taking it to the dishwasher.

"Wherever she's from, someone must be missing her by now." Dean scooped up Gucci from the floor, flipped him onto his back, and cuddled him like a baby. The small terrier looked downright tiny nestled in Dean's bulky arms and hands but was happy for the belly rubs, stretching out to give Dean access to as much of his furry belly as possible.

"She told Lynn she was staying at The Seascape.

Also, she might have a reservation tonight for table five at La Truffe Noire," Karla added.

"Those are good leads, La-la," Dean praised. "Well done." He sighed and placed Gucci on the floor, then pulled out his notebook, and opened it on the table in front of him. "I'll send an officer to Shearlock Combs first thing tomorrow to talk to the staff there. Maybe she paid with a credit card or told them some identifying information." He jotted notes as he spoke. "I'll follow up with The Seascape Hotel and La Truffe Noire tonight after I visit Lynn and take her statement." He jerked his head sideways toward the cottage next door where Lynn lived.

Karla and Lynn lived in side-by-side twin cottages on the grounds of their ancestral home, Bellcroft. Karla lived in Mirabel, the cottage where Grandma May had lived and where Karla had grown up.

Lynn lived in Bellflower, the cottage next door. Karla had both cottages gutted and renovated after Grandma May's death. On the inside, Mirabel no longer resembled Karla's childhood home, but she still found comfort in being there.

"Since you still haven't officially identified Leila, I assume Clark didn't find her missing suitcase or purse on The Aquaholic?"

"There's no sign of the missing items," Dean confirmed. "At this point, we're assuming someone tossed them overboard, and no one witnessed it." He shook his head. "But if that's the case, there should be video footage of the luggage falling into the water."

"There are security cameras on the yacht?"

"Not inside," Dean clarified. "There are only two cameras inside the yacht. One pointed at Damien's office door, and one pointed at Caitlin's office door. Damien considers the rest of the yacht his personal residence and won't allow cameras. But there are several cameras on the outside of the yacht, and one of those should have picked up the falling luggage."

"Unless whoever disposed of the luggage is familiar with The Aquaholic's security details and knew about a blind spot where the cameras wouldn't capture the luggage," Karla suggested.

"If there's a blind spot, we haven't found it, La-la." He sat back in the chair and rubbed his hand across his grey flattop. "Max'n'cheese noticed something interesting when she was processing the suitcase we found in the cabin. There were no tags on any of Jennifer-Leila's clothing. Someone had cut them all out. Why do you suppose someone would do that?"

Karla shrugged one shoulder. "Maybe she had sensory issues? Tags can be itchy and annoying."

"Maybe."

Dean's nod gave Karla the impression that he wasn't convinced sensory issues could be the reason.

"You're not convinced?" she asked.

"It's possible, La-la, but considering Damien Casey's job, reputation, and connections, we have to be open to the possibility that Jennifer-Leila was working on someone's behalf."

"Like a spy or something?"

"Maybe." Dean's nod was more convincing this time. "Someone could have sent her to find out information about Damien Casey, or maybe even to hurt him."

"She could also be a rabid Saskian," Karla countered. "Or a jersey chaser. Or a deranged mega yacht enthusiast."

"You're right." Dean held the backs of his hands against his shoulders in a placating gesture. "I'm just saying, until we figure out the dead woman's identity and why she was in that cabin, we must consider every possibility. Even the most unlikely ones."

Karla gave Dean an insulated bag with heaping servings of Rosalie's chicken and salad for Max and Rob. He promised to deliver both containers tonight. As he left to interview Lynn, he asked Karla not to be too hard on her mother for discussing Just Task Me! business with strangers in a salon.

"She's so proud of you, La-la. She loves to brag about your accomplishments," Dean pleaded in Lynn's defence. "And she's excited that you're letting her work with you. She's trying to make amends. To be a better mother and for you to get to know each other better."

"OK, Dad, I'll keep it in mind."

"Also, because of Lynn's indiscretion, we have two solid clues that could lead us to Jennifer-Leila's true identity, the hotel room and the restaurant reservation."

Karla had always been in awe of Dean's lack of animosity toward Lynn. He seemed to harbour no ill will toward the woman who declined his proposal, had his baby, left their baby with her mother, then disappeared from their lives for almost forty years. Granted, Lynn had been eighteen years old and overwhelmed, but forty years was a long time to avoid your responsibilities and not own up to your mistakes.

"I'm not going to fire her, Dad." Karla rolled her eyes.

"I'm glad to hear it."

Dean kissed his daughter's forehead, said goodbye to his granddog, and trudged across the shared lawn to Lynn's cottage.

SEVEN

A TOUPEE IN A TORNADO

THE DAY after the murder

Karla's phone was already chiming and vibrating before she'd even opened her eyes. While she slept, news about the mysterious woman's death flew through Bellbrook faster than a toupee in a tornado. Dean and his officers had kept the situation quiet as long as they could, but there was no disputing the locals who, with their own eyes, had seen Rob and her coroner's assistant removing the deceased woman's bagged body from the police boat and loading it into the back of the town's white, unmarked coroner's van.

With a lack of any actual facts to guide them, the people of Bellbrook were using their collective imagination to conjure explanations for her presence on the yacht and her mysterious death. She snuck aboard to burgle the wealthy occupants. She was an international spy who snuck onto the yacht to plant covert surveillance devices and monitor Damien's top secret political meetings and conversations. She was an obsessed Saskian. She was stalking Ben. She was Damien's mistress. As she and Gucci walked their regular morning route, Karla scrolled through her phone, hoping someone had suggested a theory that hadn't already occurred to her. They hadn't.

Karla's phone chimed with a message from Rob.

ROB

Time for a quick coffee?

KARLA

I always have time for my best friend!

ROB

Déjà Brew? Fifteen minutes?

I can walk to Déjà Brew in fifteen minutes, Karla challenged herself. *It'll be my daily cardio.*

KARLA

Meet you there.

"Good morning, Karla," Harry bellowed as he emerged from the thicket with his Irish wolfhound, Clancy.

"Good morning, Harry." Karla smiled, and Gucci tugged on his red leather Valentino leash and collar with silver studs, desperate to get close enough for Harry to pet him and within sniffing distance of his friend, Clancy.

"I thought you'd left for the day," Harry said. "Your car's not here."

"It's not fixed yet," Karla explained, rubbing Clancy's furry grey head. "The dealership is still waiting for a part. Hopefully it'll be ready today."

"I'm heading into town if you need a lift," Harry offered, crouched down to Gucci's level with the excited pup resting his front paws on Harry's knee for balance, bouncing on his hind legs, and wagging his tail like a fan.

"It's fine," Karla said. "I don't mind walking, but thank you. There's no need to interrupt your day."

"It's not an interruption, Karla," Harry insisted. "I offered because I want to do it." He furrowed his thick silver brows and shook his index finger at her. "We've talked about this. You don't have to be so self-sufficient. Accepting help is not a sign of weakness," he lectured. "When people offer to do something for you and you decline, you deny them the opportunity to do something nice for someone else and to feel good about it."

Harry was right, and Karla hated it. She had lived in the city for so long that she had gotten used to being independent. Old habits died hard. She had embraced the anonymity that the busy city provided and took pride in not asking for help. But now that she was back in Bellbrook, where even the most mundane task was turned into a community effort, she struggled to relax her high standards of independence, cede a bit of the control she loved to have, and accept that cooperation was a way of life here and helping was as much for the helper's benefit as it was for the person receiving the help.

"Thank you, Harry, I appreciate the offer." Karla smiled. "I just need to drop off Gucci at home first."

"Perfect," Harry replied with a triumphant grin. "I'll take Clancy home, grab my keys, and pick you up in a few minutes." Harry looked at Clancy who had loped away to sniff and pee on a nearby tree. "C'mon Clancy!" He let out a shrill whistle and scratched his bushy silver beard. "Let's go."

Harry and Clancy disappeared into the trees toward his cabin.

Harry Kincaid had lived in the gamekeeper's cabin on the Bellcroft estate his entire life. He was the same age as Lynn and Dean; the three of them had gone to school together. Harry took over the gamekeeper position from his father, who had taken it over from his father before him. Being Bellcroft's gamekeeper was kind of Harry's family business. Except Harry had never married or had children. There were no more Kincaids waiting in the wings to inherit the game-keeper position when Harry was ready to retire.

Karla didn't like to think about Harry retiring. She couldn't imagine Bellcroft without him. He was as much a part of Bellcroft as the manor house, the trees, and the ocean. Karla had never known Bellcroft without Harry, nor had she known Harry without Bellcroft. Harry wasn't family in the traditional sense, but he was the only doting uncle Karla had ever known. He had been part of her everyday life growing up. Harry doted on her like the favourite niece he'd never had. Every week, he had joined Grandma May, Karla, and Rosalie for Sunday dinner. He'd built a treehouse for Karla and Rob in the woods on the estate. And a tree swing. In the winter, he had made a small skating rink for her and her friends in Grandma May's backyard. When she was little, Harry had often walked her to and from school, teaching her about the trees and local wildlife that also lived on the estate grounds. When she'd been old enough to walk by herself, he'd sometimes snuck her a secret five-dollar bill so she and Rob could get ice cream or candy after school. "But don't spoil your dinner," he warned as he slipped her the folded bill, "or your grandmother will tear a strip off me."

THE INSIDE of Harry's beloved old white pickup truck smelled like motor oil and fake pine. Karla resisted the urge to tear the pine-tree-shaped air freshener from the rear-view mirror and toss it out the window as they drove. The cracked leather bench seat was scorching from the heat of the summer sun, even though it was still quite early in the morning.

"You already knew she was dead, didn't you?" Harry

shouted to be heard over the sound of the wind rushing past their open windows.

Karla nodded. "Dad asked me not to say anything," she explained.

"Who was she?" Harry asked, his thick head of silver hair blowing in the breeze. "Why was she there?"

"No one knows," Karla admitted. "It's a mystery."

Karla told Harry how they had discovered the deceased woman's body inside a locked cabin and how some of her luggage had disappeared. She knew Harry wouldn't say anything. Karla trusted him implicitly. Along with Max and Rob. She could tell him anything in confidence. She told him how the dead woman conned her way aboard the yacht by pretending to be Karla's assistant.

"Don't be too harsh on Lynn," Harry said, echoing Dean's pleas from the night before. "She's trying her best to build a relationship with you."

"So everyone keeps saying," Karla mumbled.

"She just gets a little carried away sometimes," he reasoned.

They pulled up in front of Déjà Brew.

"I'm going to the garden centre to check on the river rocks I ordered for the path through the cutting garden," Harry informed her. "They were supposed to be delivered yesterday. Then I'll tidy up and meet you there when you bring your client to view the venue."

"Thanks, Harry." Karla didn't have to tell Harry how important Saskia and Ben's tour was. He knew this was their big chance to make Bellcroft a successful event venue again and earn back the money they had invested in renovations. "She's so excited to visit Bellcroft. I get the feeling that, if she likes what she sees, it's a done deal, and Saskia and Ben will book their wedding with us."

"I knew you'd make Bellcroft a huge success." He winked with a knowing grin. "I couldn't have made a better investment."

When Karla found out she had inherited Bellcroft from Grandma May, she knew she had inherited a money pit. The main building was derelict, having spiraled into a state of disrepair after Grandma May ran out of money to maintain the mansion over three decades ago. Karla had to decide whether to sink her entire net worth, and then some, into repairs and renovations, or to subdivide the large estate and sell the oceanside manor house. Desperate to hang on to her family's ancestral home, Karla devoted all her resources to restoring and renovating the historical building and re-landscaping the grounds. Eager to support the venture and restore the estate to its former glory, Lynn contributed her inheritance from Grandma May to the renovation, and Harry donated what Karla suspected was most, if not all, of his retirement savings. She'd tried to talk him out of it, but Harry was adamant he wanted to help gentrify the estate and insisted he could afford it because he had never paid rent—living rent free in the gamekeeper's cabin was a benefit of his position.

Karla unbuckled her seatbelt and thanked Harry for the lift. As she tugged the door handle to open the truck door, Harry said, "Just shoot me a text when you need a lift back to Bellcroft, and I'll pick you up."

"Thanks, Harry," Karla said, fighting the instinct to decline his offer. She didn't need another lecture before she'd had her first cup of coffee.

EIGHT

G'DAY LADIES

"OVER HERE." Rob stood and waved her hand over her head.

Karla smiled, made a beeline for Rob, and slid into the small two-person booth in the corner of the bustling cafe.

"Americano with a dash of simple syrup." Rob slid a steaming mug of coffee toward her.

"Thank you." Karla smiled, grateful for a best friend who always knew her order. "It's busy here today." She wrapped her hands around the wide mug and lifted it toward her mouth.

"Nothing gets Bellbrookians out and about like an unsolved murder."

"Murder?" Karla froze, the mug almost touching her lips. "Leila was murdered?"

"You haven't heard?" Rob asked, leaning in closer and lowering her voice to a whisper. "I assumed Dean or Max would have told you."

"I haven't spoken to them yet today," Karla said.

"They worked late last night, caught a few hours' sleep, and were back at work by the crack of dawn." Rob stifled a yawn. "I worked late with them. Thank goodness Josie is at her dad's this week."

Josie was Rob's nine-year-old daughter. Identical to Rob but smaller in scale and wiser than most adults. Rob and her soon-to-be-ex-husband shared fifty-fifty custody, an arrangement that Rob was still struggling to get used to.

"Are you sure Leila was murdered?" Karla understood that murder was a possibility, but she had clung to the hope that Rob would discover the dead woman had an underlying medical condition, or she had suffered some sort of fatal and unfortunate accident near the bathtub. "How do you know?" Karla asked, then finally took her first sip of coffee, swallowed, and inhaled deeply, savouring the moment the first drop of caffeine touched her soul.

"I haven't completed the full autopsy," Rob said as a professional disclaimer, "but there's enough evidence so far to suggest her death was homicide."

Karla leaned in until their heads were almost pressed together above the centre of the small table. "Like what?" she whispered.

"First, we found hairs on the bed that, upon initial examination, match the hairs on Leila's head." She looked around to make sure no one was eavesdropping.

"I'm just waiting for the lab to confirm that they came from the victim."

"So, at some point, Leila was on the bed," Karla concluded, remembering the rumpled white duvet cover and disturbed accent cushions. "That doesn't mean she was murdered, right? Maybe she just rested on the bed for a few minutes. To be fair, the bed looked really inviting. I wouldn't blame her for being tempted to try it out."

"There was evidence of conjunctival and facial petechiae," Rob added.

"What's that in non-doctor speak?" Karla asked, sipping her Americano.

"Red, pin-prick sized spots that occur when tiny capillaries in the eyes and face rupture due to increased pressure on the veins in the head because something has obstructed the airways," Rob explained.

"She had red spots on her skin from the small veins in her head and eyes bursting under the pressure of being suffocated?" Karla paraphrased. *What a painful, terrifying way to die.* She placed her mug on the table as a wave of nausea roiled in her belly.

"Or strangled," Rob said. "But in this case, I suspect the petechial hemorrhage was likely caused by suffocation."

"How can you tell the difference?"

"I retrieved fibres from Leila's throat," Rob disclosed in the quietest whisper possible. "I'm waiting for the lab to get back to me, but I'd be willing to bet the fibres from Leila's throat will match the fibres from one of the pillows on the bed."

"Someone smothered her with a pillow?" Karla asked, matching her friend's volume.

Rob nodded. "I'm doing the autopsy as soon as we finish our coffee," Rob said, "but I don't expect to find water in her lungs." She sat upright and sipped her iced coffee. "But I will look for any other fibres that she may have inhaled while her killer suffocated her. The cause of death is a hold back," Rob explained. "Dean wants the public to believe that the police think she died by drowning. He's hoping the true cause of death will help the police find the killer."

"Got it." Karla nodded. "So, you suspect she died on the bed and someone moved her dead body to the bathtub?"

"Dead people can't move themselves," Rob replied with a half shrug.

"Why move the body?" Karla asked. "Why didn't the murderer kill her in the bathtub, if that's where they wanted us to find her, or just leave her on the bed? The killer had to take extra time to move her. Every extra moment they spent at the crime scene increased their chance of getting caught in the act."

"I don't think this murder was premeditated," Rob surmised. "It seems more like a spur-of-the-moment murder. A crime of passion or panic or something. It's like the killer panicked when Leila died and staged the scene, hoping investigators would presume it was suicide or an unfortunate accident."

They sat in silence. Karla sipped her coffee, processing the information Rob had just divulged.

"Why didn't the killer toss the body over the balcony?" Rob wondered aloud. "It would have delayed finding her and possibly destroyed some of the evidence."

"There are cameras," Karla explained. "According to Dean, there are cameras covering the outside of the yacht. Cameras that would have captured Leila's body going overboard. He thinks the killer knew about the cameras. That's why he was so certain Leila's missing luggage was somewhere on the yacht. It would have been difficult to get it off the yacht without being caught on camera or seen by someone."

"Good morning, ladies."

Suddenly, four women clad in yoga leggings and tank tops surrounded their small corner table.

"Good morning," Karla and Rob responded in stereo.

"Is it true you were on the yacht yesterday, Karla?" asked the brunette ponytail who, judging by her position in the middle of the group and her confident posture, was The Head Poser.

"Yes," Karla admitted. It wasn't like she could lie. Lots of people, including The Posers, would have seen her climbing on board the yacht tender yesterday, then disembarking the police boat hours later.

The Posers were a group of alleged yoga enthusiasts who, as far as Karla could tell, spent most of their time occupying the centre table at Déjà Brew, monitoring the comings and goings of their fellow townsfolk and discussing other people's business. They always wore yoga gear, had rolled up yoga mats poking out of their backpacks and gym bags, yet no one had ever actually seen them at Om Sweet Om, the local yoga studio. Regardless of their methods, their information was almost always accurate, and they had been known to use their powers for good when necessary to quash harmful and inaccurate gossip.

"Did you see her?" The blonde reverse bob leaned in, eager to hear Karla's response. "The dead woman," she clarified. "Were you there when they found her?"

"Sort of," Karla admitted, trying to answer the question without giving away too much information for fear of compromising the police investigation. "I can't talk about it," she explained. "You know, client confidentiality, police confidentiality, so many confidentialities."

"Did you meet her before she died?" asked the pixie cut with frosted tips. "Did you speak to her?"

"Look at the time!" Rob announced, checking her smartwatch and interrupting the conversation before Karla could answer the curious Poser. Every day, Rob changed the band on her smart watch to match her scrubs. Today she wore olive-green scrubs with an olive watch band. "I have to go." She stood up, forcing the Posers to take a step back from the table.

"Me too," Karla announced, following her best friend's lead.

"You're so close, even your outfits match," pointed out the brunette shoulder-length shag. "Did you two coordinate your outfits on purpose?"

Karla looked at her sleeveless, muted olive blouse tucked into a pair of slim darker olive-green cigarette pants that ended just above her ankle, and her strappy gold stiletto sandals, and realized that she and Rob looked like a sample card for shades of olive-green paint.

"Total fluke," Karla assured The Poser.

The Posers suddenly became distracted, perking up like curious meerkats and forgetting all about Karla and Rob's matching wardrobe choices. They whispered to each other, pointing excitedly to something, or someone, outside.

"There he is!" The blonde reverse bob bounced on the balls of her feet and grabbed the brunette ponytail by the arm.

"He's back," observed the brunette ponytail, narrowing her eyes.

"He's so handsome!" said the brunette shoulder-length shag.

"Who?" Rob asked, straining to look through the window at what, or who, had The Posers in a tizzy.

"The tall, good-looking Australian guy," replied the brunette shoulder-length shag cut. "He's come in here three days in a row now. He's one of the yacht people.

He usually wears a white uniform like Richard Gere in *An Officer And A Gentleman.*"

"That scene where Richard Gere sweeps Debra Winger off her feet in the factory…"

"Captain Peterson?" Karla mumbled, peering through the window, squinting to see through The Posers' reflections in the clean glass.

"Who?" demanded the brunette ponytail. "What did you say his name was?"

"I'm not sure," Karla muttered, uncertain if the man who had The Posers swooning was the same man who drove her to The Aquaholic yesterday and unlocked the cabin where they'd found Leila's body.

It *could* have been Captain Peterson, but it was difficult to tell for sure. His back was to the window, and he wasn't wearing his crisp white captain's uniform—the only outfit Karla had ever seen him in. Instead, he wore a pair of slim, straight leg khaki pants, a royal blue short-sleeved golf shirt and brown leather sandals. He was tanned enough to be Captain Peterson. He was the right height, build, and had similar short, neat, salt-and-pepper hair. His head was bobbing and his hands were gesticulating, but his body blocked whomever he was conversing with.

"He's come in here every day since The Aquaholic arrived. This will be his third visit to Déjà Brew," said the blonde reverse bob. "He always orders a doppio and a cup of ice water to go." She stared at the man's back with a mischievous glint in her eye. The corner of her mouth twitched slightly upward. "Then as he leaves, he looks right at us, smiles, winks, and says, 'G'day, ladies,' in his hot Aussie accent." She fanned herself.

"Yesterday, he looked at our yoga mats and said, 'I bet you ladies are flexible, aren't you?' I almost fainted," added the pixie cut with frosted tips amid a fit of giggles.

"I wouldn't mind showing him how flexible I am," purred the brunette ponytail.

"Stop!"

"You're baaad,"

"Me too!"

The other posers gushed in response, giggling and playfully swatting their flirty friend.

"He can't be *that* cute," Rob argued. "I mean, no one is *that* hot."

Captain Peterson turned his head and looked toward the cafe.

"Never mind." Rob nodded. "I was wrong. He looks like he just fell out of an issue of GQ magazine."

"He's the captain of The Aquaholic," Karla confirmed.

The reverse blonde pouted. "That means he's leaving soon. I was hoping he'd be around a while."

Captain Peterson turned back to his unknown conversation partner and shifted his weight. He held a crumpled paper bag in his hand. He nodded to the nearby garbage pail, lined up his shot, and lobbed the bag into the can. Karla heard whomever he was speaking to cheer when the bag made it into the basket.

Hey, I know that laugh! Karla thought.

Captain Peterson was fidgeting with his wedding band when he stepped to the side and pivoted his body just enough that, instead of his back, Karla could now make out his profile—and the person to whom he was speaking.

"Lynn?" Rob blurted, pointing out the window. "Is he talking to Lynn?"

"Mother?" Karla couldn't believe her eyes.

"Way to go, Lynn." The brunette ponytail gave Karla's mother an impressed nod.

Lynn laughed, tossing back her head, and flicking her hair behind her shoulder with one hand, while *almost* placing her manicured fingertips on Captain Peterson's tanned, muscular forearm with the other. Was Lynn flirting with a client? Not that Captain Peterson was a client, but he was the employee of a client which, as far as Karla was concerned, crossed the same professional line. *I guess we need to discuss professional distance.*

NINE

OOPSIE DAISY

"I WASN'T FLIRTING, LOVE," Lynn defended herself against Karla's accusation. "I was being polite to a tourist. He stopped me and asked for directions." She gestured vaguely around them. "Bellbrook is a summer tourist town, in case you've forgotten." She shook her index finger at Karla. "Tourism is the backbone of our local economy, remember? The last thing Bellbrook needs is online reviews claiming the townsfolk are rude and unhelpful."

Karla only had Lynn's side of the story to consider since Captain Peterson had disappeared by the time Karla had woven her way through the busy cafe and made her way to the sidewalk outside.

"Directions to where?" Karla crossed her arms in front of her chest and tapped the toe of her stiletto sandal on the sidewalk.

"He was looking for a florist, love," Lynn replied

with a small huff. "He wants to send flowers to his wife. She has a big presentation at work or something, and he wants her to know he's thinking about her even though he can't be there."

"He works for Damien Casey," Karla whispered, "which means he's practically a client of Just Task Me!. We don't fraternize with clients or their employees. Ever."

"I told you, love, we weren't flirting." Lynn seemed downright exasperated with the accusation. "He asked if I could recommend a local florist that could send flowers internationally. I recommended Oopsie Daisy." She pointed toward the local florist. "In fact, when he told me he worked on The Aquaholic, I introduced myself as a Just Task Me! employee and offered to take care of his order for him." She shrugged her right shoulder. "May as well. I'm going to Oopsie Daisy, anyway." She held up her cell phone. "He texted me his wife's name, address, and the message he'd like to include on the card." She pocketed her phone. "Her favourite flowers are white or blush ranunculuses. I always thought they were called Persian Buttercups, but Captain Peterson says they're called ranunculuses." She shrugged. "He would know, I guess. He says he and his wife have a garden full of them."

"From inside Déjà Brew, it looked like you were flirting."

"No one was flirting," Lynn insisted. "Trust me, if Captain Peterson was flirting, he wouldn't have spent five minutes waxing lyrical about his wonderful wife. He wears a wedding ring, for goodness' sake. Just because a man is ruggedly handsome and speaks with a sultry Australian accent doesn't mean I can't control myself. What kind of woman do you think I am?"

The truth was, Karla didn't really know what kind of woman Lynn was. They had spent so little time together that Karla and Lynn hardly knew each other at all. She knew Lynn rarely stayed in one place longer than a few months. She knew Lynn had mentioned a new boyfriend practically every time she phoned or sent a postcard to Grandma May. She knew Lynn had handed over Karla to the loving care of Grandma May when she was just a few months old, left Bellbrook, and almost never looked back. And thanks to Rosalie and Harry's constant reminders, she knew that when Karla was born, Lynn had been a terrified, over-whelmed eighteen-year-old girl trying to cope as best as she could under tremendous stress.

Karla relaxed her stance and added, "I'm sorry if I got it wrong." She gave Lynn a small, apologetic smile. "I guess I'm still uneasy after yesterday when you told Leila and Jennifer more than you should about The Aquaholic and my professional connection to Damien Casey."

"I promised you that won't happen again," Lynn reminded her. "And it won't."

"Why are you going to Oopsie Daisy?" Karla asked.

"You said you were going there, anyway, before Captain Peterson asked about a florist."

"I thought I'd pick up flowers for the manor house," Lynn replied. "We want the venue looking its best for Saskia and Ben's private tour today. After the florist, I'm heading to Rosalie's house to pick up a charcuterie board, blueberry cheesecake bites, and a few other nibbles she made to help Saskia and Ben feel welcome."

"Good idea," Karla commended. "Saskia has chosen a palette of muted fall colours for the wedding. I'll text you a link to her mood board."

"I'll check what muted fall colours the florist has in stock." Lynn nodded.

Karla and Lynn said goodbye, and Lynn headed toward the florist farther up Main Street.

"Are you OK?" Rob asked.

Karla turned to Rob, having forgotten that her best friend had followed her outside.

"Yes," Karla replied. "I'm fine. But I suspect Lynn might be growing bored with Bellbrook's small-town lifestyle. It wouldn't surprise me if she hitched her trailer to the next visiting cowboy and rode out of town."

"I'm not so sure," Rob disagreed. "Lynn seems to have different priorities now. She's trying really hard to build a life here and build a relationship with you."

"Time will tell," Karla said, hoping to end the conversation.

"Besides, if anyone was flirting, it was probably him. You heard The Posers talking about how friendly he was with them and that comment he made about how flexible they were." Rob checked the time on her watch. "I have an autopsy to perform," she reminded Karla.

"I'll walk with you," Karla offered.

They strode down Main Street, soaking up the mid-morning sun and pausing occasionally to look in a store window, or smile and say hi to a friend or neighbour.

"Karla!"

Karla and Rob stopped, searching for the source of Karla's name.

"Woohoo! Karla!"

Caitlin Lopez jogged toward them, impressively fast for someone wearing heels.

"I'll call you after I finish the autopsy," Rob mumbled.

"Good luck," Karla said, unsure if those were the appropriate words of encouragement for a doctor about to perform an autopsy.

Rob continued walking, and Karla waited while Caitlin's long strides closed the gap between them.

"You left this in my cabin yesterday." A breathless Caitlin thrusted the wide-brimmed sun hat toward Karla.

"Thank you," Karla said, taking the hat. "You didn't have to deliver it. I would have been happy to pick it up next time I visit the yacht."

"It's sunny today," Caitlin reasoned. "I thought you might need it."

"Thank you." Karla smiled. "I appreciate it."

"No problem," Caitlin said. "I came to shore with Captain Peterson. This town is so small that I figured there was a good chance we'd bump into each other." She shrugged. "If I didn't run into you, I would've taken it back to The Aquaholic and asked Saskia or Ben to give it to you at Bellcroft later."

"You and Damien aren't coming to Bellcroft with them?" Karla asked.

"We'd love to," Caitlin replied, "and Damien wishes he could be there too, but something came up at work, and now we have back-to-back video meetings all afternoon."

"I'm glad we bumped into each other," Karla said. "I wanted to apologize for yesterday. Max and I didn't mean to offend you when we asked if you and Damien were more than colleagues. Max's interest was purely professional. And I want you to know that, had your answer been different, I wouldn't have judged you or betrayed your confidence."

"Thank you, Karla," said Caitlin as they strode along Main Street, heading towards the waterfront. "Since we're exchanging apologies, I'm sorry for suggesting you were responsible for bringing the dead woman on board. I know now that she was just pretending to be your assistant. Max visited the yacht this morning with an update. It turns out you and Leila didn't know each other, and she lied about her credentials to get on board."

"I wasn't offended," Karla said. "None of us was sure what to think. The whole situation was weird and scary."

"Damien trusts you, and I trust Damien's judgement," Caitlin said. "You've always been discreet and reliable, and that's good enough for me." She sighed and appeared to steel herself for what she was about to say next. "For the record, Damien and I have a strictly professional relationship. We're friendly and sometimes enjoy each other's company outside of work, but we've never been intimate. I'm *very* happy just being his friend."

"You've never been tempted?" Karla asked. "Damien's good looking. Smart. Charming. He gives off strong alpha-male energy. And you guys spend months at a time together on his gorgeous yacht."

"Not tempted," Caitlin retorted with a chuckle. "I'm a *very* big believer in keeping my personal life separate from my professional life." There was a brief pause before she added, "So you didn't ask about my relationship with Damien because of anything Max might have seen when she flipped through my planner?"

Karla hated lying. The twinge of shame when she did it made her whole body uncomfortable. As far as Karla was concerned, withholding information was just as much a lie as actually saying something untruthful. Like not admitting that Max wasn't the only person who saw the contents of Caitlin's planner, and not confessing that Karla herself had been peering over Max's shoulder and saw pages of doodles where Caitlin had practiced signing her name as Caitlin Casey, with hearts and multiple variations of her pretend signature.

"If Max had questions about something in your planner, she would have asked." Karla watched her feet as she spoke to avoid eye contact with Caitlin. "I'm relieved we didn't upset you," she continued, directing the conversation away from Caitlin's planner. "I have a lot of professional respect for you, and I'd hate to offend you."

"You didn't offend me," Caitlin insisted. "I was in shock. Finding an intruder, dead, in my home, up the hall from where I sleep, freaked me out. I've never found a dead body before."

"It would freak out anyone," Karla reassured her.

"And I was frantic with worry about Saskia. I wanted to go to her cabin and make sure she was OK, but there was a cop in the hall who made everyone stay inside their cabins until the police finished interviewing everyone and collecting evidence."

"Why were you frantic about Saskia?" Karla asked.

"Did you read the unauthorized biography that Saskia's former nanny wrote?"

"The one that came out when Saskia was little?" Karla clarified. "The one that was released after Damien won the custody battle? I read it years ago but hardly remember it."

Karla had only been working for Damien for a few years. She had read the book as research but couldn't remember most of it. Damien had neither contributed to the book nor sanctioned it, so she placed little credibility in the accuracy of its details.

"During the height of the custody dispute, Saskia found her mother floating in a bathtub," Caitlin reminded her. "She survived, but only because Saskia and the nanny got to her just in time."

Karla stopped dead in her tracks. "I'd forgotten about that," she said, recalling the passage from the book. "It was true?"

Caitlin nodded.

Saskia had been six years old. She'd been spending a week at her mother's Manhattan penthouse as per the temporary custody arrangement issued by the judge presiding over the custody case. The nanny had left the penthouse to pick up young Saskia from a nearby birthday party. While she was gone, Saskia's mother washed down an assortment of prescription and non-prescription painkillers with a few shots of tequila. She then thought it would be a good idea to take a bath. It wasn't. Saskia and the nanny returned to the penthouse just in time to save the woman's life. According to the nanny's version of events, it was Saskia who found her mother floating in the bathtub. Miraculously, Saskia's mother survived and agreed to go to rehab. Again. She spent the next several years in and out of various rehab facilities, all at Damien's expense. Damien's legal team had used the incident to arrange an emergency court hearing where the judge awarded full physical custody of young Saskia to Damien.

"That event traumatized Saskia," Caitlin revealed. "I had only worked with Damien for a few years at that point, but I remember how the bathtub incident affected her. That girl was haunted by what had happened. She was like a different child after. Before she left to visit her mother, Saskia was her usual energetic, fun, playful self. When she came back, she was different. She hardly slept and had nightmares when she did. She was sullen and anxious. She clung to Damien like she was scared she'd never see him again if he left the room. The nanny had to teach her to use the shower because she trembled and cried if Damien or the nanny tried to coax her into a bath." Caitlin looked over her shoulder, then leaned in, and whispered, "One time, I found her floating her doll in a sink full of water. She'd hold it under the water, then pull it out, and save it. She would do this for hours."

"Oh, my!" Karla said. "I've never heard about any of this. It wasn't in the book, and I don't recall hearing about it in the press."

"It wasn't," Caitlin said. "Damien and the nanny were protective of Saskia. Damien did everything he could to keep Saskia's struggle out of the media. Even the nanny didn't include the aftermath in her book. Everyone thinks Damien loved the media attention around the custody battle. They think he used the court of public opinion to poison gossipmongers against Saskia's mother, but he didn't. Damien hates the press. Always has."

"But Saskia's livelihood depends on the media," Karla pointed out. "She uses the paparazzi to her advantage. She's one of the most photographed celebrities in the world."

"Damien hates it," Caitlin claimed. "He thinks the media exploits his daughter, and he thinks her fans— The Saskians—are dangerous. But he's a good, loving dad. He supports Saskia's choices regardless of how he feels about them. He doesn't confide in many people, but he confides in me, regularly, about how much he hates the media and Saskia's fans."

Could he hate them enough to kill them? Karla asked herself. What if Leila was paparazzi or a crazed fan who snuck aboard the yacht to get close to Saskia? Could Damien have found her and become so enraged at the breach of privacy and decency that he killed her to protect his daughter?

The women resumed their lazy pace along Main Street.

"Have you spoken to Saskia?" Karla asked. "Did finding Leila's body in the bathtub trigger her past trauma?"

"I spoke to her last night, and I saw her at breakfast this morning. She was a little quieter than normal but seemed fine. She didn't see the body," Caitlin revealed. "Everyone else saw it except her. Damien and Ben took turns comforting her and keeping her away from the bathroom. Damien told us not to discuss it in her presence. He's afraid the details might upset her and bring back memories of her mother. We've all complied. No one wants to upset Saskia. But just because she didn't see it doesn't mean it didn't affect her. One good thing that has come from this is that Saskia and Ben have stopped arguing. He's being super attentive and doting on her now."

"Saskia and Ben had been arguing?" Karla asked. "They seem so affectionate and in love. What were they arguing about?"

"Same old argument they always have," Caitlin replied. "Girls throw themselves at Ben and Saskia gets jealous."

"Why would she be jealous?" Karla asked. "Saskia is gorgeous, famous, and it's obvious Ben adores her."

"I love Saskia and I love Ben," Caitlin reasoned. "I don't want to say anything negative about them. They're great people, but they've had relationship issues, just like any other couple."

"What sort of issues?" Karla pressed.

"Ben's a bit of a flirt," Caitlin disclosed. "Girls approach him all the time when he's out in public. They take selfies with him and try to insinuate they know him better than they should. Fans send him flirty messages and intimate photos on social media. Saskia is a pretty confident woman, but early in their relationship, Ben cheated, and she still struggles with it. Sometimes, she accuses him of cheating. He gets angry. She reminds him why she's insecure. He tells her to get over it and threatens to cancel the wedding if she can't trust him."

"I had no idea," Karla said, stunned at how dramatic life on the yacht seemed to be. If Caitlin was telling the truth, it certainly wasn't the peaceful, idyllic life of leisure that Damien had led her to believe. "Do you think Ben cheats on Saskia?"

"No." Caitlin's response was confident and without hesitation. "Ben loves Saskia, but he gets frustrated because he's not as comfortable as her with living in the spotlight. She's monetized their relationship, and he doesn't like that. Their life together appears perfect and easy, but creating that illusion is a full-time job."

"Maybe today isn't the best day to look at wedding venues," Karla thought out loud. "Maybe I should call Saskia and offer to reschedule. You know, give her some time and space to deal with what happened on the yacht yesterday."

"No! Don't do that!" Caitlin protested. "Saskia *needs* to find a wedding venue. They're getting married in three months. This wedding is a huge media event. Saskia and Ben have contractual obligations. She has secured sponsors, sold rights to the first interview and first photos, and world-famous fashion designers have donated their time to design the dresses and suits in exchange for the publicity. This wedding *must* happen. Her image and reputation depend on it. Saskia Casey is proud, like her dad. Her image means everything to her, and she would do anything to preserve it."

Would Saskia Casey kill to preserve her image? Karla wondered to herself. If Leila had sneaked aboard for a secret rendezvous with Ben, or even if she was just hoping to meet her celebrity crush in person, could that pressure, so close to the wedding, have been enough to push Saskia over the edge of reason? Did Saskia kill Leila in a fit of jealous rage and leave her in a tub of water just like she had found her mother twenty years earlier?

TEN

KISSES AND AFFECTION, NOT
BARKS AND BITES

KARLA MADE a point of always arriving everywhere before her clients and never making them wait. Therefore, she and Gucci arrived at the manor house before Saskia and Ben. The walk wasn't long, but the midday summer sun was hot, leaving both Karla and Gucci parched by the time they reached their destination.

"You should have sent me a text," Lynn said when she saw her panting daughter and granddog. "I would've picked you up."

"It was time for Gucci's midday walk, anyway," Karla replied, relishing the central air conditioning and focussing on the silver lining in her car situation.

Karla's car still wasn't ready. The dealership had sent her a wordy apologetic text message along with a guarantee that it would be ready tomorrow and, to compensate for the inconvenience, offered a free maintenance visit when it was time to install the snow tires and winterize her car.

"Saskia and Ben aren't here yet." Harry stated the obvious as he placed a bowl of water on the kitchen floor for Gucci. "Do you usually bring Gooch when you meet with clients?" he asked, rubbing the terrier's small head and slipping him a piece of homemade jerky from his pocket. "I left Clancy at home. I didn't know this was a dog friendly meeting."

"Gucci's here by special request," Karla replied. "Saskia has seen him during our video chats and wants to meet him in person. She even sent a text message reminding me to bring him." She found a drinking glass in the cupboard and poured herself a glass of cool water from the dispenser built into the stainless-steel commercial fridge. "The place looks incredible," she said before gulping down half the glass.

"Thanks, love," A hint of a blush peeked through Lynn's perfectly applied makeup. "The theme was simple elegance. I used Saskia's mood board for inspiration."

"Saskia will love it." Karla smiled.

Rosalie's creative, albeit larger than necessary, char-cuterie board, platters of various sweet treats, a bottle of champagne—in a chiller—and several stemless, crystal champagne glasses adorned the large white quartz kitchen island. Lynn had stocked the small beer fridge in the butler's pantry with Ben's preferred brands. Simple yet striking floral arrangements adorned the kitchen table, island, and various accent tables through the main floor.

It wasn't long before Ben and Saskia pulled up in two chauffeur-driven black, electric SUVs.

The first SUV carried Saskia, Ben, and a huge bodyguard who looked too big to fit in the vehicle. He positioned himself next to the passenger door, standing at attention with his feet hip width apart, his hands clasped in front of him, and his shoulders squared. He was like a human statue. His serious expression didn't move, and Karla couldn't tell what he was looking at behind his mirrored aviator sunglasses.

The second SUV carried the head of Saskia's Social Media Strategy Team, Saskia's head stylist, and four outfit changes, complete with shoes and makeup.

"Welcome to Bellcroft." Karla beamed as she greeted them.

"Is this Gucci?" Saskia ignored Karla's welcome and focussed on the excited terrier who was pulling on his leash, whimpering and desperate to reach his new best friend. "He's even more adorable in person." Saskia crouched down, and her voluminous maxi skirt billowed around her. Not understanding about expensive designer clothes, Gucci trampled all over it, trying to reach her face and give her kisses. Saskia didn't mind. She seemed to love Gucci as much as he loved her. She turned her head and looked up at her fiancé. "We should invite Gucci to the wedding, babe!"

"As a guest?" Ben sounded mortified at the idea. He

pressed his back against the SUV as though, if he moved a muscle, Gucci would attack him. He would, but with kisses and affection, not barks and bites.

"Actually," Karla said, "he has a little tuxedo. He wore it last Halloween."

Saskia gasped and inspiration twinkled in her amber eyes. "We could have a tux made for him," she suggested. "To match the groomsmen." She looked at Ben again. "He could go from table to table during the reception, greeting the guests. Like a little host. What do you think, babe?"

"I think we should tour the venue first," Ben suggested, creeping sideways until he ran out of car to press himself against, then slinking past Gucci before running into the house.

"Does Ben have allergies?" Karla asked Saskia. "Gucci is hypoallergenic."

"He's not allergic," Saskia explained with an eye roll. "He's scared. He's terrified of dogs. When Ben was growing up, his grandmother had a mean miniature schnauzer that would always corner him and growl."

"Oh," Karla said. "That's too bad." *It's a good thing Clancy isn't here. Ben would be downright terrified of the huge hound.*

"It's devastating," Saskia corrected. "I've always wanted a dog. Since I knew dogs existed. My dad would never let me get one because we travel so much and spend so much time at sea. I would've asked my mother, but she could barely look after herself, never mind keep a pet alive." She sighed, gave Gucci a final head-to-tail stroke, returned to standing, and straightened her skirt. "I guess I'll never have a dog. Ben is too terrified of them. He was a sweaty, anxious mess the whole time that police dog, Clark, was sniffing around The Aquaholic yesterday."

Interesting, thought Karla. *Was Ben a mess because he was afraid of Clark or because he was afraid of what Clark might find?*

The social media strategist and stylist were wandering around the front of the mansion, whispering among themselves, pointing, and snapping photos on their cell phones.

"They're scoping out potential locations for photo-shoots," Saskia explained, gesturing to her employees. "And, if it's all right with you, we might take a few staged photos today to tease my followers leading up to the wedding?"

She phrased it as a statement, but Saskia's voice intonated at the end like it was a question, so Karla nodded her approval. "Maybe you should see the rest of the estate first," she suggested.

The tour went well. Saskia loved every room more than the one before it. Her excitement about getting married at Bellcroft was palpable. She was full of ideas and enthusiasm about Bellcroft's potential to be the best wedding venue ever. By the end of the tour, she had decided that the bridal party and groomsmen would stay at the manor house in the days leading up to the wedding.

"What about our parents, babe?" Ben asked.

"My dad will stay on his yacht." Saskia shrugged. "Your parents can stay with him, and we'll book every hotel room in town for everyone else."

Ben nodded. He hadn't said much during the tour but seemed pleased that his fiancée was happy. He kept a constant, watchful eye on Gucci and maintained a safe distance from the excitable pup.

By the time the tour was over, Saskia had decided they would host the rehearsal dinner in the dining room and invite the immediate family to a special breakfast the morning after the wedding.

They would hold the reception in the ballroom, and the doors to the huge patio would be open so the party could spill outside. Karla made notes about securing a tent and heaters because October nights this close to the ocean could be chilly and unpredictable.

Her strategist pointed out that the outbuildings would be perfect command centres for the media outlets who had purchased the rights to photograph and video parts of the ceremony and reception. The stylist had a few concerns about lighting.

"Send me a list of your requirements," Harry said in his role as project manager for the massive renovation project. "When our contractor, Griff, gets back to town at the end of the month, we'll see what we can do to accommodate them."

There was that name again. Karla knew Griff hadn't left town for good, but she had hoped his absence would be an out-of-sight-out-of-mind situation. She had looked forward to not being distracted by him for a while. So much for that.

"Other than the beautiful gardens and the patio, are there options for good outdoor photos?" the social media strategist asked.

"Wait until you see the waterfront," Karla said with a knowing grin. "Follow me."

Karla led Saskia, the stylist, and the social media strategist to the private waterfront behind the manor house.

Saskia was speechless until she wasn't. "This is it," she declared. "This is where I want Ben and I to exchange our vows. Right here next to the water."

The stylist and strategist jumped in to manage Saskia's expectations about weather, tides, and other unknown variables that might disrupt her plan. Their quick intervention and coordinated effort gave Karla the impression that managing Saskia's expectations was, perhaps, the biggest part of their jobs.

"Would you mind if we took some photos near the water?" Saskia asked. "I want to hype up my followers with a few photos of the venue as the wedding gets closer."

"Sure," Karla replied.

The stylist and strategist left them and rushed to

retrieve Saskia's wardrobe changes, makeup, and hair products from the car.

"Changing my look gives the illusion that we took the photos at different times," Saskia explained to Karla. "This way we have enough photos for several days, and my followers think each photo is new."

"You and Ben should come back tonight and tour the estate after dark," Karla said as she and Saskia ambled back toward the house with Saskia holding Gucci's leash. "It's beautiful when it's lit up. You'll get some great nighttime photos."

"That's a good idea," Saskia agreed. "My dad can come with us. He wanted to come this afternoon, but Caitlin scheduled a bunch of meetings." She rolled her eyes and let out a frustrated huff. "Apparently, something urgent came up."

"I heard," Karla said. "I offered to reschedule the viewing again, but Caitlin didn't think it was a good idea. She said how disappointed she and Damien were that they couldn't be here."

"I bet she did," Saskia muttered. "That's what she wants you to think."

"Why would she lie about wanting to visit your wedding venue?"

"Caitlin saw an opportunity to get my dad all to herself and took it," Saskia replied. "With me and Ben off the yacht, and a bunch of the crew taking time off to visit the town, they're practically alone on The Aquaholic. Caitlin loves having all my father's attention. It wouldn't surprise me if those urgent meetings were suddenly cancelled or rescheduled at the last minute."

Is this why Caitlin had been so insistent that Karla not postpone today's tour? Was she really worried about how close the wedding was, or did she want Damien to herself? Karla was getting the impression that Caitlin and Saskia didn't have the warm, friendly relationship that Caitlin had led her to believe.

"May I ask a personal question?" Karla asked when they stopped so Gucci could sniff a rock.

Saskia nodded. "Shoot."

"Are Caitlin and Damien a couple?"

"She wishes!" A small snort escaped when Saskia tried not to laugh. "My dad doesn't see Caitlin as a romantic option, and it drives her crazy," Saskia said. "Caitlin Lopez has been in love with my father for as long as I can remember. He's too oblivious to see it, but to everyone else it's as obvious as the cigar in his shirt pocket and a bit sad." As they neared the house, Saskia handed Gucci's leash back to Karla. "She uses me to get to him," Saskia revealed. "I like Caitlin, but she tries too hard to be my friend, my mother-figure, whatever she thinks will impress my dad."

"Is it possible that Caitlin wants to be your friend and mother-figure because she likes you? I mean... she's known you since you were little," Karla suggested in Caitlin's defense.

"You don't know Caitlin very well, do you?" Saskia's tone suggested that Karla didn't know Caitlin at all.

"She's clever and calculating," Saskia continued. "She hates other women having access to my dad. Sometimes I feel like she's jealous of *me,* and I'm his daughter. I'm surprised she's so friendly with you. She must not think you're a threat. I bet she told you she's 'married to her job and *very* happy just being Damien's friend.'"

Saskia's impression of Caitlin was dead on, like she had practiced mimicking her father's executive assistant.

"Word for word," Karla replied absently, her mind replaying the interactions she had with Caitlin on Main Street earlier that day and aboard the yacht the previous afternoon.

"She also mentioned how generous Damien is as an employer. Apparently, he invites Caitlin's sister to visit the yacht and even spends time with her sister's kids so Caitlin and her sister can spend time together."

"Caitlin's sister hasn't visited The Aquaholic in ages," Saskia said, shaking her head. "They fought about something a couple of years ago, and as far as I know, Caitlin has only seen her sister, niece, and nephew at a couple of family events since then."

I know Caitlin's Tell!

"Have you ever noticed that there are no female crew members on The Aquaholic?" Saskia asked, interrupting Karla's revelation.

"Now that you mention it," Karla replied, wracking

her brain to recall whether she had encountered a female crew member during her visit.

"It's not a coincidence, you know," Saskia said. "Caitlin is responsible for hiring. She only hires men. Less competition for my dad's attention."

"Maybe women are underrepresented in the yacht industry," Karla hypothesized, still hoping to redeem Caitlin with Saskia.

"I'm pretty sure that's not the reason," Saskia said dismissively. "She also sabotages his relationships. She's the reason he's alone. If he's interested in a woman, she makes it too difficult for him to spend time with her. She books meetings that coincide with their dates, she makes travel arrangements that keep him away from whoever he's interested in." Saskia looked Karla in the eye. "If Caitlin Lopez can't have my father, no one can. But my dad doesn't see it, and even if he did, he's so dependent on her that he probably couldn't do anything about it."

Did Caitlin kill Leila? Jealousy is a powerful motive. Maybe Leila was a special friend of Damien's, and Caitlin found out.

"She was pretty worried about you after we found the body yesterday," Karla said as a segue. "If you need to talk to someone, a professional, I can arrange it. No one else would need to know, if that's what you want. Just say the word and I'll make it happen." Karla knew Rob could recommend someone qualified and discreet.

They stopped walking as they reached the door to the house.

"Thank you, but there's no need to worry," Saskia retorted. "I'm fine." She shrugged one shoulder. "I know everyone is waiting for me to have some kind of breakdown because the dead woman was in the bathtub, like when I found my mother twenty years ago, but I'm fine. Finding that Leila woman was nothing like finding my mother. I'm older now. More mature. I can handle it better. Also, my mother was floating face down and wearing a bathrobe, Leila was face up and fully dressed. It wasn't the same at all."

How do you know what Leila's body looked like? Karla wondered to herself but didn't ask out loud. Didn't Caitlin say that Saskia never saw Leila's body? Didn't she say that Ben and Damien were sure to keep her away from the bathroom? Didn't she also say that Damien had asked everyone not to discuss the details with Saskia for fear of triggering her past trauma? Did someone who was at the scene go against Damien's wishes, or did Saskia see Leila's lifeless body firsthand? But how could she when Damien and Ben had tasked themselves with keeping her away from the bathroom? Could Saskia have seen Leila's body earlier? Was Saskia the reason Leila was floating in the tub?

ELEVEN

HAPPY SPOUSE, HAPPY HOUSE

BEN WAS RELIEVED to find out his presence was not required at Saskia's impromptu seaside photo shoot. He was also relieved when Saskia asked if Gucci could be in the photos with her. Apparently, the distance between the manor house and the waterfront was sufficient for Ben to relax and not be on high alert for Gucci's sudden movements.

"My followers will love Gucci," Saskia gushed as she picked him up and cuddled him close to her face. "And the Versace bikini I'm planning to wear for the first shoot matches Gucci's Versace collar and leash! It's too perfect! He's like a mini-me!"

Euphoric at the coincidence and still snuggling Gucci, Saskia disappeared into a nearby powder room where her stylist and strategist had set up an impromptu dressing area.

"Would you like to visit the waterfront, Ben?" Karla

asked. "We can make it there and back before Saskia and Gucci get there for their photoshoot."

"No thank you, Ma'—Karla. It's not necessary. If Saskia's happy, I'm happy."

"Happy spouse, happy house, amirite?" Harry teased.

"Yes you are, sir—I mean Harry."

"Where's Lynn?" Karla asked.

"She took a bottle of water to the bodyguard," Ben replied.

"He's still standing there." Harry jerked his thumb toward the front of the house. "He hasn't moved a muscle. I've been watching him through the window. He's a human statue."

"I got a nod out of him," Lynn announced, sweeping into the kitchen. "He didn't move though, so I just put the water on the hood of the SUV. He's sweating. There are beads of sweat on his forehead, and he won't even move to wipe them."

"He's fine," Ben assured them. "That's just how he is."

This seemed acceptable as everyone nodded.

"Where's my granddog?" asked Lynn, searching around her feet for the pup who was usually so happy to see her that he would attack her knees whenever she entered the room.

Karla told Lynn about Gucci's photo shoot with Saskia down by the water.

Lynn volunteered to join them in case anyone

needed anything, grabbed a few bottles of water and a small bowl for Gucci, zipped them into an insulated bag, and left.

While Karla was showing Saskia the waterfront, Ben and Harry bonded over Ben's short athletic career.

"Karla, did you know that in his rookie year, Ben rushed the ball 330 times for 1,601 yards and nine touchdowns?"

"Really?" Karla asked, nodding and hoping she looked sufficiently impressed. "That's amazing." She had no idea what the numbers meant. "That must have been a record?"

"Oh, it was," Harry replied on Ben's behalf. "He also caught 40 passes for 305 yards and scored on three receptions."

"Wow," Karla said, understanding nothing that Harry had just said. "That's incredible." *Right?*

"Thank you," Ben replied, equal parts proud of his achievements and embarrassed that Harry was making such a big deal of them. "I'm not the only former athlete on The Aquaholic," Ben said, directing the conversation away from himself. "Captain Peterson was a lock for Queensland County."

"Rugby," Harry explained for Karla's benefit. "He played professional Rugby in Australia." He opened two cans of beer and handed one to Ben.

Karla nodded. "I didn't know that."

"I'm sure he told Lynn all about his athleticism

when he flirted with her earlier," Harry muttered under his breath before taking a swig of beer.

Is Harry jealous? Based on things she'd overheard growing up, Karla had always suspected that Harry had a crush on Lynn when they were in high school, but it never occurred to her that Harry still had feelings for her mother.

"They weren't flirting," Karla defended. "Mother was helping him with something. Besides, how did you hear about it?"

"Can't keep secrets in this town, Karla," Harry reminded her, then took another swig of beer.

"The hedge trimmer is here," Harry said, lifting his chin toward the window. "I need to have a word with him." He placed his beer can on the counter. "The hedges were way too short last time." He looked from Karla to Ben. "Excuse me. I'll be right back."

"It looks like Saskia and I are getting married at Bellcroft," Ben announced, filling in the silence left by Harry's departure. "This is the most excited she's been about any venue, and we've visited dozens of potential venues on four continents since we got engaged."

"Which venue was your favourite?" Karla asked.

"They're all the same to me," Ben admitted. "This wedding business is exhausting, and I can't wait to get married so it will be over." He laughed. "But seriously, as long as Saskia gets the wedding of her dreams, I'll be happy wherever we get married."

"She wants to come back tonight," Karla said. "The estate is beautiful at night with the gardens and the manor house lit up. She wants Damien to see it too." She sighed. "I hope he likes it as much as Saskia."

"Damien Casey will say and do anything to make his daughter happy," Ben said in a reassuring tone. "I'm sure he'll love Bellcroft, but even if he doesn't, he wouldn't say anything that might dampen Saskia's enthusiasm about it."

"Are you and Damien close?" Karla asked. "Caitlin mentioned how you worked together yesterday to comfort Saskia when we found you-know-who in the you-know-what." She was purposely vague, just in case someone was nearby.

"Are sons-in-law ever close to their fathers-in-law?" Damien asked, answering her question with a question.

"Some are, yes," Karla replied. "How about you and Damien?"

"We're friendly, but not friends, if you know what I mean."

Karla nodded, understanding exactly what Ben meant. There was a difference between being friends and being friendly.

"The only thing we really have in common is Saskia," Ben continued. "We both love her and always put her first. Beyond that, we don't interact much. Saskia says he likes me, but I feel like he just tolerates me, so she'll be happy. He has a way of making me feel... inadequate. Like I don't belong in the same room as him. It's hard to explain." He swished the beer around inside the can. "Let's just say, in Damien Casey's opinion, no one would be good enough for his daughter. She could marry Prince Charming, and he'd still think she settled."

"Did something happen between you?" Karla asked. "Do you think there's a reason Damien might not like you?"

"It was something that happened when Saskia and I first got together," he said, shaking his head dismissively.

"I'd heard you cheated on her," Karla said cautiously, hoping she didn't just offend the future son-in-law of one of her biggest clients.

"I never cheated," Ben insisted with more emotion than Karla had ever witnessed from him. "Yes, that girl and I had a fling, but it was before Saskia and I even met. That girl sold her story and her photos of us to a tabloid, and the tabloid insinuated the photos were recent. They weren't. I hooked up with that jersey chaser months before I ever laid eyes on Saskia."

"Does Saskia know that?" Karla asked.

"I've told her," Ben said in a tone that sounded defeated. "I showed her my text messages with that girl to prove that we'd stopped texting two months before Saskia and I met." He sighed. "It doesn't make sense, but Saskia is insecure. On the outside, she's confident and self-assured, but deep down, she worries people don't like her, and she's afraid that everyone will leave her."

I can't imagine why, Karla thought to herself sarcastically. *Her mother left her repeatedly because of addiction, and her father sent her to boarding schools for most of her childhood and left her in the care of nannies when she wasn't at school.*

"There's nothing I wouldn't do for Saskia," Ben claimed. "I love her more than anything."

Would you kill for her? Karla wondered. *Or would you kill with her?*

What if Leila had snuck aboard The Aquaholic to rendezvous with Ben, Saskia found out, and Ben killed Leila to prove his love and devotion to Saskia? Or maybe they killed her together. Or... what if Saskia killed Leila, and Ben helped cover up the crime?

"Did Saskia see Leila's body in the tub?" Karla's whisper was so quiet that Ben had to lean in and put his ear near her mouth.

"No, she didn't," he insisted, shaking his head as he leaned away. "I know for a fact that she didn't see *the body*." He mouthed the words *the body*.

"She described it to me," Karla challenged. "In detail."

Ben shook his head harder. "Damien and I made sure she didn't see that scene. He even texted everyone after and told us not to talk to her about the details. He was afraid she would freak out."

"Did Saskia ask you about it?" Karla asked. "Did she ask you to describe the scene in the washroom?"

"Yes," Ben admitted.

"Did you tell her?"

"Do you think I'd be stupid enough to defy Damien Casey?" It was a rhetorical question.

TWELVE

TECHNICAL DIFFICULTIES

KARLA INHERITED her propensity for punctuality from her father, Dean. Neither of them could stand being late and went out of their way to always be on time, or better yet, a little early. Karla wasn't sure what motivated Dean to strive for perpetual promptness, but anxiety was her motivation. The thought of being late filled her with a nagging mental and physical unease that she would do anything to avoid. So, she did not complain, and was a tad relieved, when she and Dean arrived at the dock fifteen minutes before the yacht tender was due to pick them up.

"Thanks for driving me to the marina, Dad," Karla said as she unbuckled the seatbelt and opened the door of Dean's patrol car.

"No problem, La-la. I have an appointment with Damien Casey on The Aquaholic, so I was coming here, anyway."

"About the murder case?"

"Strangely, no," Dean replied. "He wants to talk about security for Saskia's wedding. He's worried the Bellbrook Police Department doesn't have the resources or experience to handle such a large, high-profile event."

"I can help set him straight."

"Thanks, La-la. But I think I can handle him." Dean locked the patrol car, and they walked toward the dock where the tender was supposed to pick them up. "Why are you going to the yacht?"

"Dinner," Karla replied. "Saskia and Ben invited me. They want to discuss the wedding, then I'm taking them back to Bellcroft for a nighttime tour."

Standing on the dock, waiting for the tender to pick them up, Karla replied to emails on her phone while Dean paced. He paced one side of the dock, then the other, all the while keeping his eyes peeled on the water sloshing below.

"Looking for something?" Karla asked, knowing full well that Dean was scoping the area for a sign of Leila's missing bags.

"Leila's missing luggage is really gnawing at me," Dean admitted. "I've had divers search around the yacht and dispatched marine officers to search the water. We've even asked the fishing boats to keep their eyes open for anything suspicious. It's like the luggage just disappeared into thin air." Dean brought his fingertips together and made a mock *poof* with them.

"The ocean's pretty big, Dad," Karla said, trying to console him. "Maybe the luggage sank and hasn't resurfaced yet. Or maybe the wind changed and carried it in a different direction."

"We should have found something by now," he muttered. "Something's not right with this situation, and I can't stand not knowing what."

"Did you follow up with La Truffe Noire and The Seascape hotel?" she asked, hoping to refocus her father on the more productive parts of the investigation.

"There was no reservation at La Truffe Noir," Dean said. "The maître'd said the restaurant was fully booked last night. This is one of their busiest months. Last night's reservations were booked weeks in advance. He said he would've known if there had been a last-minute cancellation and someone else filled it. Also, none of the reservations for a table for two included a woman named either Leila or Jennifer. I even asked him to check for a reservation in Lynn's name in case the dead woman pretended to be someone else again."

"So the restaurant was a dead end," Karla sympathized.

"Yeah," Dean agreed. "It would've been great if she had booked a table and given them her and her boyfriend's names for the reservation."

"She might have paid Shearlock Combs with a credit card," Karla suggested hopefully.

"Cash," Dean said, shaking his head.

"What about the hotel?"

"She had a room at The Seascape," Dean confirmed. "But she didn't have a reservation. She showed up yesterday morning and took the only room they had available. The clerk remembered her because he told her how lucky she was to get a room this time of year, without a reservation. Lucky for her, a guest had to check out early and left the night before."

"Did you search her hotel room?"

Dean nodded. "Yes, but we found nothing useful. Just her fingerprints, and the fingerprints of a few hotel employees. The hotel's security cameras captured her arriving with her luggage—two bright pink rolling suitcases and a large, brown, crossbody bag, just like everyone said. The cameras also captured Leila leaving at a time that coincided with her visit to Shearlock Combs, returning after her visit to the salon, then footage of her leaving the hotel with her luggage a short time later, presumably to sneak aboard The Aquaholic. She didn't check out, but she took all her luggage. Was she planning to leave for good? Or was she planning to come back but was permanently delayed?" Dean wondered aloud with a shrug. "We may never know."

"Leila must have provided a credit card when she registered," Karla said. "You can't stay in a hotel without giving them a credit card number to keep on file."

"Can you believe their computer was down when she checked in?" Dean closed his eyes and shook his head in disbelief. "'Technical difficulties,' the hotel manager called it. I call it a comedy of errors. The clerk who registered her was a summer student. He's new and didn't know how to process a credit card without the computer, so he didn't take it. He told her they would call her room and ask for her credit card information when the computer system was fixed."

"Oh my," Karla said. "That's too bad."

"That's what the hotel manager said. He also said the correct procedure was to photocopy Leila's ID and credit card, input them into the system when it started working again, then destroy the photocopies. But the clerk didn't know that, and they were short staffed yesterday, so they never got Leila's credit card. They also require guests to provide details about their vehicles, so I'd hoped to get the make, model, and plate number, but she arrived by cab. She told the clerk she came straight from the airport. I've assigned an officer to contact cab companies and try to track down the car that picked up Leila from the airport. It's like searching for a needle in a haystack." He let out a heavy breath.

"But they confirmed her name was Leila?" Karla asked.

"Yes," Dean replied. "She checked in as Leila Grant and gave them her cell phone number."

"That's a significant lead."

"It's a burner," Dean said, dashing her hope. "She probably picked it up at a convenience store somewhere and used it on a pay-as-you-go basis." He looked at Karla and squinted into the sun behind her. "Why would Leila have a burner phone?"

"Maybe because of her boyfriend?" Karla suggested. "Leila told Lynn and Jennifer that she and her boyfriend had to be discreet during their visits because his job involves security, or something, and he needs to stay below the radar."

"Whose radar?" Dean asked, exasperated. "She also told Lynn and Jennifer that her boyfriend was only in town for a few days. For all we know, he's already gone." Dean used the toe of his huge black police shoe to kick a leaf from the dock into the water. "Max mentioned you figured out Caitlin Lopez's Tell."

Karla nodded. "She uses the word, very, and exaggerates it *very* much. Now that I know her Tell, it's *very* easy to tell that she lied to Max and I about her feelings for Damien and, for whatever reason, lied to us about her relationship with her sister. Basically, Caitlin is in love with Damien and no longer has a close relationship with her sister."

"Interesting." Dean's notebook was out, and he made notes as Karla spoke.

"I think I figured out Ben Underwood's Tell too," she continued. "His is interesting and less common than the usual Tells. He avoids lying by either changing the subject or answering a question with another question."

"Can you give me an example, La-la?"

"When I asked him if he disobeyed Damien, which I suspect he did, he replied with, 'Do I look stupid enough to defy Damien Casey?' He also did it when I asked him if he and Damien were close. They're not, by the way, but Ben says they have an understanding based on their mutual love for Saskia."

The tender's arrival interrupted their conversation. Dean flipped shut his notebook, clicked his pen, and returned them to his pocket.

This yacht tender was identical to the one that took Karla from shore to ship yesterday, except this one had white leather upholstery instead of tan.

"Is this a different boat?" she asked the deckhand who was driving. "The tender that picked me up yesterday had white leather seats."

"Good eye," said the young deckhand. "The Aqua-holic has two tenders in this size. The only difference is the upholstery colour."

"There are two yacht tenders?" Dean asked in his authoritative cop voice. "I was only aware of the one Damien offered to let us use. No one mentioned another one." He looked at Karla. "I don't think Clark searched it."

The deckhand shrugged at Dean's comment, shifted the speedboat into gear, and steered it away from the dock.

Karla lurched when the boat moved. She grabbed the back of the white leather bench seat for support. *I should sit down before I fall and break a heel or a hip.* She used the seatback to steady herself as she maneuvered to the front of the leather bench seat. As she lowered her weight onto the seat, it shifted beneath her. Something wasn't secure. The seat cushion wasn't flat. She stood to adjust the seat and noticed it was sticking up at a weird angle. She lifted the cushion to figure out what was causing the issue and hopefully fix it. To her surprise, the bench seat was an actual bench. The seat lifted to allow for hidden storage inside. Peering through the narrow gap between the bench seat and the base, Karla glimpsed something pink and shiny. *No!* she thought to herself. *It can't be!* She cracked open the bench just enough to glimpse its contents. *Bingo!*

"Dad."

Dean's back was to her. He couldn't hear her over the rushing water smacking against the side of the boat and the wind in their ears.

"DAD!" Karla shouted, tugging on the back of his size XL black Bellbrook PD golf shirt.

Dean turned.

She pointed at the bench cushion. When Dean fixed his focus on the upholstered white leather, she opened the bench to reveal a hot pink hard-side rolling suitcase that was just a hair too tall to allow the lid to close properly.

Dean's jaw dropped, and his eyes widened. He looked at Karla, then back at the poorly hidden luggage.

"What the h—" A seagull swooped low between them, its squawk drowning out the last syllable of Dean's sentence.

THIRTEEN

AN UNEXPECTED OFFER

BY THE TIME they arrived at the yacht, Dean had already sent text messages summoning officers to process the recovered luggage and perform a thorough search of both yacht tenders.

"I knew it," Dean said, staring at his phone screen with crinkled brows. "Clark didn't search either tender."

"Welcome back." Caitlin's smile disappeared when she saw the open bench seat on the boat. She blinked fast, and her jaw dropped. "Is that?" She looked from Karla to Dean. "Is that the dead woman's missing luggage?"

"It appears so," Dean replied.

"Has it been there this whole time?" she asked.

"Your guess is as good as mine," Dean said with a sigh.

Caitlin shook her head. "But she and I rode to The

Aquaholic on the other tender. Jennifer, Leila, whatever she's called was never on this tender." She turned her attention to her cell phone. "I'd better let Damien know what's happening."

Dean offered Karla his hand as she stepped off the boat and onto the yacht. "La-la, can you tell Damien that I'll contact him to reschedule our chat? I'll have to stay here and guard the luggage until my officers arrive to process it."

"Sure, Dad," Karla replied, then looked at Caitlin. "Didn't you mention something about a log where the crew records the names and times for everyone who comes and goes from The Aquaholic?"

"The tender logs." Caitlin nodded.

"I'm going to need those logs, please," Dean said.

"Of course," Caitlin replied and gave the deckhand a curt nod.

Dean fidgeted, shifted his weight, and stared at the luggage like it was taunting him.

Karla could sense his frustration about having to wait to open the bags until his officers arrived, and they could examine the evidence methodically, following protocols.

"Here you go, Chief Sheridan." The deckhand handed a black notebook to Dean.

"This is it?" he asked. "Everything on this yacht is state of the art. I was expecting the logs to be online or something."

"We're kind of old school in some ways," Caitlin

explained.

"It's for both tenders," the deckhand explained. "Each tender used to have its own log, but one of them was full, and no one replaced it, so now we record everything for both tenders in one book."

Dean opened the notebook and flipped to the last few pages. Karla stood next to him, scanning the logs of departures and arrivals.

"There are missing entries," Karla exclaimed.

"I think you'll find these logs are accurate and up-to-date," Caitlin disputed. "Damien is a stickler for accurate record keeping."

"According to The Posers, Captain Peterson has visited Déjà Brew three times in the past three days," Karla said, pointing to the entries for the past two days.

"That's right," Caitlin agreed. "I went with him. We really like that little coffee place in town."

"Those trips aren't recorded here," Karla said.

"Are you sure?" Confusion clouded Caitlin's face as she sidled up to Dean's other side and scanned the open notebook over his arm. "You're right. My trips ashore aren't logged at all." She reached around Dean's large arm and flipped back a few pages. "No one has logged my arrivals or departures for weeks." She gave the deckhand an accusatory scowl.

"We aren't as diligent with the tender logs as we used to be," admitted the deckhand. "Most of us forget to fill them in." He shrugged. "It's mostly just family and crew members coming and going from the yacht.

We try to be sure and log outsiders who visit, but aside from that, we've gotten pretty lazy with the logs."

"They're useless," Dean declared, shutting the notebook.

"Anyone could have snuck aboard." Caitlin pointed out.

"Not with all the cameras that are mounted to the outside of the ship," Dean reminded her. "We've analyzed the security footage from the outside cameras, and no unknown boats or people approached the yacht around the time of the murder."

"Are you suggesting one of us is the killer?" Caitlin asked, wide eyed.

Had Caitlin seriously not considered the possibility that the killer could be someone who worked and lived aboard the yacht? Or was this her attempt to make Dean believe she was too naïve to commit murder?

"The killer is not aboard this ship," Damien's elongated southern drawl arrived two steps before he did. "I trust everyone who lives and works on The Aquaholic. Most of them have been loyal employees for many years. They're like family." He brought the stub of his cigar to his mouth and took a long pull.

"That's right," Caitlin said, positioning herself next to her boss. "On top of that, we employ the services of a *very* expensive security company. They do *very* thorough and *very* frequent background checks on all the crew and staff."

"How thorough?" Dean asked.

"*Very,*" Caitlin reiterated.

Dean shot Karla a knowing look, then said to Caitlin, "I'd like to read their most recent report."

"Of course," Caitlin said. "I can email it to you next time I'm near my computer."

"Mr. Casey, remind me again where you were yesterday before you met with Karla on the upper deck?" Dean asked.

"I was in my office." He turned his head slightly to the right and made side-eye contact with Dean. "I was discussing wedding details and seating arrangements with my daughter. It's all she wants to talk about these days." He chuckled and brought the cigar stump to his mouth. "I swear I've told your officers this a hundred times already. This is why I'm skeptical that your little police department has what it takes to handle the demands of a wedding as big as Saskia's." He puffed the cigar again.

Karla gave Dean a discreet headshake.

"I don't believe you," Dean challenged.

"Excuse me?" Damien straightened his spine and puffed out his chest. "Why on earth not?"

"First, your daughter's fiance, Ben, also claims he was with her all morning. But in her statement, Saskia claims she was alone in her cabin yesterday morning while you were at work, and Ben was at the onboard gym."

Who was lying, Damien, Ben, or Saskia? Are Damien and Ben lying to give Saskia an alibi? Ben said that he and Damien have a common interest in always protecting her.

"*Pshaw*." Damien dismissed the evidence. "Saskia is easily confused, Chief. Yesterday was rather traumatic for her. I'm sure you understand how she might have mixed things up in her mind."

"Second, Karla doesn't believe you, and if she says you're lying, you're lying."

"Karla?" Damien pivoted his body and glared at her. "Please explain."

"You do this when you lie," Karla said, turning her head slightly to the right and giving Damien the side-eye.

"Poppycock," he said with a nervous chuckle. "That's not evidence. That's nonsense." He huffed and held out his finished cigar butt. The deckhand hurried over to take it from him.

"Prove it," Caitlin challenged with her hands on her hips and one arched brow. "What do I do when I lie?"

"You exaggerate the word *very* when you lie," Karla continued, proving her point. "In fact, you hardly use the word *very* at all, except when you lie."

Damien gave Caitlin a scrutinizing stare, nodding. "Now that you mention it, you're right about Caitlin." He narrowed his gaze and changed his focus to Karla. "How did you figure that out?"

"Karla's a human lie detector," Dean explained, but it sounded more like a brag. "I've never known her to be wrong."

"I might not have been wrong about whether someone is lying," Karla clarified, "but I can't determine everyone's Tell. So sometimes, I can't say for sure that they're lying. I might have a hunch that someone is lying, but unless I can figure out their Tell, I don't have a specific behaviour to support my hunch."

"How?" Damien asked again, laser-focussed on Karla. "I need to understand *how*."

"The short version is, I have a knack for noticing people's *very* small micro expressions and patterns." She added the *very* on purpose, hoping it might lighten the mood. It didn't. In fact, it seemed to irritate Caitlin, who rolled her eyes at the reference. "I also have the ability to recognize patterns quickly and isolate behaviours that don't match someone's established patterns."

"Dr. Mayhew suspects that Karla's special gift is a byproduct of her ADHD and SPS."

"Dad!" Karla hissed under her breath so he'd stop discussing her neurodivergence.

"Sorry," Dean mouthed to his daughter.

"Fascinating." Damien put his arm around Karla's shoulder. "Tell me more," he urged, guiding her away from the tenders and deeper into the yacht.

"Damien!" Caitlin called, jogging after them. "The senator is waiting for your response to his email. We need to go over the reply I drafted."

"The senator will have to wait, Caitlin," he said over his shoulder. "This is more important."

FOURTEEN

IF LOOKS COULD KILL

AS THEY WALKED, Karla told Damien about Rob's theory that Karla's ADHD, combined with her suspected Sensory Processing Sensitivity made her hyperaware of even the smallest stimuli, and how she could process it in a short amount of time.

"Basically, my brain is like a super-fast computer with a tiny memory," she said with a half laugh.

"Are there lots of people like you?" Damien asked, leading them to the upper deck where they had met for iced tea the previous afternoon.

"I don't know," Karla replied. "I've never met anyone else who can detect lies, but it's not something I usually talk about."

"So, your special skill is a secret?"

"Not exactly," Karla replied. "I just don't disclose it to everyone I meet. It seems to make people uncomfortable."

"I'm not uncomfortable," Damien assured her with a sly grin. "In fact, I'm quite intrigued."

He pulled the unlit backup cigar from his shirt pocket and slid it under his nose, inhaling its aroma, then slipped it back into his pocket.

Damien might not have been uncomfortable, but Caitlin sure was, judging by the way she kept shifting her weight, gnawing on her upper lip, and tapping her toe at least a hundred times per minute.

"I'm glad." Karla smiled. "By the way, my dad is going to want to look at the footage from the security camera outside your office."

The table was set for supper. Damien pulled out Karla's chair. She sat down, and he gently pushed her toward the table.

"No problem," Damien agreed, then looked at Caitlin. "Make sure Chief Sheridan has full access to whatever he needs to aid in his investigation."

Damien's demeanor had changed. He was calmer than usual, intensely focussed on Karla, and his voice was slower with an almost singsong quality. He wanted something from her.

"Yes, Damien." Caitlin didn't look up from her planner when she answered him.

Damien sat across from Karla and Caitlin sat next to him. The deckhand took their drink orders.

"I want you to come and work for me, Karla," Damien said out of nowhere, with the nonchalance of someone commenting on the weather.

"What?!" Karla and Caitlin blurted in stereo.

"You can't be serious, Damien." Caitlin's gaze shifted furiously back and forth between Karla and Damien.

"As serious as a heart attack."

The corner of Damien's mouth twitched into a crooked grin, and he maintained intense eye contact with Karla in a way that made her feel vulnerable and small.

She resisted the urge to cross her arms in front of her chest and draw back in retreat. Instead, swallowing hard, she took in a deep breath, pulled herself to her full seated height, and met Damien's stare with her own.

"Damien, I'm flattered—"

"Karla already has a job," Caitlin blurted, interrupting Karla's response. "She runs a successful concierge business."

"I'll pay you more than you earn now, and you won't have to deal with any of the hassles and demands that come with entrepreneurship," Damien cooed, ignoring Caitlin's protest.

"Uh—"

"Her family is here," Caitlin insisted, interrupting Karla's attempt to object on her own behalf. "And Bellcroft." Caitlin let out a frantic huff. "She has a dog for goodness' sake. Karla can't just abandon her life to work for you."

"Name your price," Damien offered, ignoring Caitlin's arguments against the idea. "I'll pay whatever you want. You'd live on The Aquaholic. You'll have a private cabin, and you can even bring that little dog of yours. The one Saskia can't stop talking about. What's his name? Armani?"

"Gucci," Karla said. "My dog's name is Gucci."

"I can hire people to help look after him. You and Gucci can travel the world and get paid handsomely for the privilege." Damien leaned forward and narrowed his gaze. "Someone with your unique skill set would be invaluable to me, Karla." He laced his hands together on the table in front of him. "You see, there's a lot of bullshitting in politics, pardon my language, and your unique skill set would give me, and my clients, a considerable tactical advantage. Do you understand what I'm saying?"

"I think I get the gist." Karla nodded.

"You would work exclusively for me. No one else," he clarified. "But working for me has its perks. You'd have the luxury of time. Enough time to do whatever you want. We'd work closely together, of course. You would have to accompany me to meetings and functions, but aside from that—"

"Perhaps we should table this discussion until after dinner." Caitlin slammed shut her planner and tucked it next to her on the chair. Her jaw was so tense, the muscles were twitching. "Saskia and Ben will be here any second, Damien, and you know how Saskia feels about you discussing business when she's trying to talk to you about the wedding."

As if on cue, Saskia and Ben arrived on the upper deck.

"I was hoping you'd bring Lynn and Gucci," Saskia said with an exaggerated pout.

Ben's body stiffened at the mention of Gucci. He scanned the deck for any sign of the spirited terrier.

"Gucci and Lynn couldn't make it, I'm afraid." Karla watched Ben's body return to its pre-Gucci relaxed state.

"She brought Chief Sheridan instead," Damien teased. "They found the dead woman's missing luggage, and now our floating paradise is being turned into a crime scene. Again."

"Is that police dog here?" Ben asked, eyeing everyone suspiciously. "The big scary one that sniffs everything?"

"Not yet, but I'm sure he'll grace us with his presence soon," Damien replied, then brought his daughter and her fiancé up-to-date on the details of the recently discovered baggage.

As Damien finished updating Saskia and Ben, the deckhand delivered the salad course. A simple mix of locally grown seasonal ingredients including leafy greens, Cabot tomatoes, sweet onions, corn, cucumber, and radishes mixed with a honey Dijon vinaigrette dressing.

Glowering at Karla, Caitlin stabbed a piece of radish and tore it off the fork with her teeth.

If looks could kill... thought Karla. *Maybe Saskia was right about Caitlin preferring not to have other women around to compete for Damien's attention. What if Leila had been the centre of Damien's attention, and Caitlin killed her to make sure Leila could never upstage her again?*

The summer salad was a scrumptious prelude to the main course of porcini-crusted filet mignon on a bed of mashed garlic potatoes with a confetti of oven-roasted grape tomatoes, leeks, and shitake mushrooms drizzled with a port wine reduction sauce.

Saskia turned the conversation to her and Ben's upcoming wedding. Karla gratefully immersed herself in wedding talk as a distraction from Caitlin's onslaught of icy glares and her aggressive use of the steak knife and fork.

Saskia was telling Damien about her plan to host the bridal party and groomsmen at the manor house in the days leading up to the wedding when her phone chimed several times in a row.

"Excuse me," Saskia said to her dinner companions. "This might be the dress designer. I've been waiting for her to get back to me about designing wraps or shrugs for the bridesmaids' dresses. Something the girls can slip over their shoulders if they get chilly at the reception." Saskia set down her fork and picked up her cell phone. As she read the screen, her serene, relaxed expression morphed into one of fear and panic. "Oh no!

The sponsors are getting cold feet!" she declared, scrolling faster. "They've heard rumours that Ben and I are involved in a police investigation into a mysterious death. Apparently, they can back out of our contract because of it. The magazine and TV show that bought the rights to cover the wedding are considering backing out too." She looked at Ben, her eyes wide with fear and confusion. "This is a disaster! What are we going to do?"

"It's OK, babe." Ben took Saskia's phone out of her hand and placed it face down on the table, then wrapped his hand around hers. "We don't need a bunch of sponsors and media coverage to get married," he reassured her. "The day is about us. The other stuff doesn't matter."

"Doesn't matter?" Saskia shouted, yanking her hand away from Ben's, her wide eyes brimming with unshed tears and horror. "What's the point of getting married if I can't share it with my followers?!" She grabbed the white linen napkin from her lap, slammed it onto her plate, and ran from the table in tears, disappearing down the stairs.

Ben motioned to follow her.

"Sit down, Son," Damien instructed.

Ben froze, half standing, half sitting.

"You know what she's like," Damien said. "If you chase after her, she'll just push herself further away. Give her time to calm down."

Ben paused, torn between his instincts and his future father-in-law. Upon choosing to heed Damien's advice, he returned his backside to his chair, pushed his plate away, and took a long sip of wine.

"Perhaps you should go after her, Damien," Caitlin suggested.

"Last time I chased after Saskia, she slammed her cabin door in my face and called me a name I will not repeat in polite company," Damien replied, cutting a piece of steak and bringing it to his mouth.

"Should I go?" Caitlin asked.

"You're the last person who should go," Damien counselled with his mouth full. "She's still mad at you for scheduling those meetings that prevented me from visiting Bellcroft with her today."

"Those meetings weren't my fault," Caitlin defended. "How was I supposed to know they'd be cancelled at the last minute?"

Saskia was right! She predicted those meetings would be mysteriously cancelled at the last minute, leaving Caitlin and Damien alone on the yacht. Did the meetings ever exist, or did Caitlin invent them as a ruse?

"Why don't I check on Saskia?" Karla offered, hoping to diffuse the tension. "When I first started Just Task Me! I planned quite a few weddings. I've had some experience calming down anxious brides." She smiled.

"Of course you have," Caitlin muttered, rolling her eyes. She pushed a piece of shitake mushroom around her plate with her fork, then stabbed it a few times for good measure.

"Are you sure you don't mind, Karla?" asked Damien. "I hate to draw you into our family drama."

"I'm happy to help," Karla replied, pushing herself away from the table.

FIFTEEN

THE STINK EYE

KARLA FOUND Saskia on a smaller deck, one level below the upper deck she'd run away from.

"There you are," Karla declared. "I've been looking everywhere for you."

Saskia was on the floor, hugging her knees to her chest and resting her back against a large white deck box Karla assumed was for storing the lounge cushions when they weren't in use.

"May I join you?" Karla asked.

Saskia said nothing but shifted over to make room in her hiding spot for Karla.

They sat in silence, staring at the vast expanse of ocean and sky in front of them. Saskia occasionally sniffled and dabbed her tears with the hem of her cream-coloured linen tunic.

Karla handed her a stack of paper napkins she had

picked up while hunting for the hiding social media star.

"You didn't have to come after me," Saskia finally said.

"It was me or Caitlin," Karla teased.

For a microsecond, amusement tugged at the corners of Saskia's mouth, and she almost smiled. "In that case, thank you for coming after me."

"No problem," Karla said.

"Why was Caitlin giving you the stink eye during dinner?" Saskia asked as she dabbed the corner of her eye with a napkin.

"You noticed?" Karla asked. "I wasn't sure if it was real or if I was imagining it."

"It was real." Saskia nodded. "I'm familiar with that stare." She let out a half chuckle. "I've been on the receiving end of Caitlin Lopez's stink eye more than once."

"Damien offered me a job," Karla revealed. "An opportunity to live on the yacht and work closely with him and his clients."

"Oooh, I wish I'd been there to see Caitlin's face when she heard that!"

"It was awkward," Karla said. "Neither of us was expecting it." She nudged Saskia's shoulder with her own. "You were right about Caitlin, by the way. She's possessive of Damien and doesn't like it when he pays attention to other women. You're very insightful."

"It doesn't take much insight when Caitlin makes

her feelings for my dad so obvious." She nodded. "I think you'd like living and working here. My dad's world is pretty cool," she added. "You'd always live in the most luxurious accommodation. You'd meet the world's most powerful people, and you'd never have to worry about paying a bill again. He and Caitlin take care of everything for everyone who works for him." Her face lit up like she had just had an epiphany. "You and I could hang out all the time. I spend a lot of time with my dad, so I'm here a lot." She hooked her arm through Karla's. "I'd have to convince Ben to get therapy for his fear of dogs, but it would be fun to have you and Gucci around. We could be like sisters." For the first time since Karla had found her, Saskia smiled.

"I have a sister," Karla reminded her.

"Right. Officer Max." Saskia nodded. "And Chief Sheridan is your dad, right?"

Karla nodded. "Lynn is my mother, Dr. Rob is my best friend, and Harry is my surrogate uncle. Bellbrook has a pretty tight hold on me."

"I get it," Saskia said. "If Lynn was my mother, I wouldn't want to leave either. When we were taking pictures at Bellcroft earlier, she lectured me about not using enough sunscreen. And between shots, she chased us around the beach with bottles of water, reminding us to stay hydrated."

"Lynn means well, but she can be a little overbearing," Karla said. "I'm sorry if she crossed a line."

"Not at all!" Saskia insisted. "I loved it! It felt

nurturing, you know?" She fidgeted with the balled-up napkin in her hand. "I'm not used to maternal attention."

"Me neither," Karla said quietly. "Until recently, Lynn and I hardly knew each other. We'd only seen each other a handful of times until last year when we both came back to Bellbrook for my grandmother's funeral. Lynn left town when I was a baby. She travelled the world while my grandmother raised me."

"Wow," Saskia sympathized. "I didn't realize we had so much in common. After the bathtub incident, I only saw my mother a couple of times a year, and those were chaperoned visits. I don't think she had any maternal instincts. I could've been sunburnt from head to toe and completely dehydrated, and my mother wouldn't even have noticed. The only people who ever cared about me were people my father hired. Nannies, tutors... even you. The only reason you're here is because my father retains your company's services."

"That's not true," Karla argued. "If I didn't want to plan your wedding, I wouldn't have agreed to. The reason I started my own business instead of working for someone else was so I would have complete control over who I work for and what jobs I accept. I'm here because I want to be. I like you, Ben, Damien"—she paused for effect— "and even Caitlin."

"I hope you accept my dad's job offer," Saskia said. "It would be nice to have someone around who likes me for me. Not because my dad is paying them or because I'm a B-list social media celebrity."

"Damien loves you for who you are. It's obvious every time he talks about you," Karla reminded her, "and Ben adores you."

"I know," Saskia admitted. "Ben is too good for me. He's so pure. It's only a matter of time before he realizes he can do better and leaves me."

"I doubt it," Karla reassured her. "Ben loves you so much he doesn't care what kind of wedding you have as long as you get married."

"Aside from Ben, my followers are the most loyal, consistent people in my life. Their approval means everything to me. If I can't share our wedding with them, I may as well not invite anyone." She sighed. "If my sponsors back out, we may as well cancel the whole thing and just elope somewhere on the down-low."

"Is that what you want?" Karla asked, hoping the answer would be a resounding no. "Do you want to ditch the big wedding and elope with Ben somewhere private? I can make that happen."

"No," Saskia replied, much to Karla's relief. "I want the huge wedding I've always dreamed about. This wedding means everything to me."

"It means a lot to me too," Karla admitted. "This is Bellcroft's first big event in almost sixty years. Everyone in Bellbrook has a vested interest in Bellcroft succeeding."

Saskia shrugged. "I guess if my sponsors pull out

because of this murder investigation, I could ask my dad to help foot the bill..."

"Let's not get ahead of ourselves," Karla said, cutting off Saskia midsentence. "When the police solve this murder, it will clear your name and Ben's. Your sponsors won't have any reason to pull their support."

"I wish I could help your dad and sister with their investigation," Saskia said. "I swear, Karla, I do not know who Leila was or why she was here."

"Is there any chance she was a Saskian?" Karla asked. "Or a jersey chaser?"

"I don't think so." Saskia shook her head. "I delay my social media posts," she explained. "It's a security measure to protect my privacy. I won't post any of the pictures we took in Bellbrook until after we leave. That way, the Saskians don't know where I am in real time."

"But yesterday you posted the selfie you took of us on the upper deck," Karla reminded her.

"It was a generic yacht photo with nothing but sea in the background. It could have been taken anywhere, anytime," Saskia reasoned. "Besides, that was right before we found the body. Leila was already dead. It's not like she recognized where I was because of that photo and snuck aboard."

"Everyone in town knows you're here, Saskia," Karla pointed out. "The Aquaholic doesn't exactly blend into its surroundings."

"Well then, I guess she could have been a Saskian,"

Saskia conceded. "But I didn't kill her. There's no way I would ever drown someone."

Does Saskia really believe that Leila drowned? Or is she going along with public opinion because saying otherwise would prove she was the killer?

"What about Ben?"

"He's a big, tall, powerful man," Saskia admitted. "But he's a gentle giant. He won't even swat a fly. He makes me do it. He closes his eyes during the gory scenes when we watch a movie. There's no way Ben could kill someone and lie to me about it."

"How did you know what Leila's body looked like?" Karla asked. "Damien and Ben said they kept you away from the scene.

"Who said I saw the body?" Saskia asked defensively, tilting her head.

"You did," Karla reminded her. "Earlier today at Bellcroft. You said Leila's death was nothing like finding your mother in the bathtub because the position of her body and outfit were different."

"Oh, yeah, I guess I did say that." Saskia squeezed her eyebrows together. "But I never saw Leila's body."

"Someone described it to you?"

Saskia nodded.

"Ben?"

Saskia nodded again.

"But Damien instructed everyone not to discuss it with you."

"Trust me, when it comes to Ben, I have more influence than my father," Saskia said.

Enough influence to convince him to kill for you?

"You really think you can save my dream wedding if the police find the killer?" Saskia asked, bringing the conversation back to her wedding.

"I promise to do everything in my power."

Karla asked Saskia to put her in touch with the sponsors and media companies.

Saskia texted her their contact details.

"Leave it with me," Karla said, hoping she sounded more confident than she was. "I'll help them see how valuable this publicity will be for them, and what a big mistake it would be if they backed out now."

"Thank you." Saskia gave Karla a small, closed-mouth smile and rose to her feet. "I feel much better."

"Are you ready to go back upstairs?" Karla asked as Saskia offered her a hand and pulled her to her feet.

"Right after I stop by my cabin and wash my face," Saskia replied. "I'll meet you up there?"

"Sounds good."

Saskia opened her arms, and Karla reciprocated. After a short, tight squeeze Saskia pulled away and asked, "You're not going to accept my dad's job offer, are you?"

"Probably not," Karla admitted. "I've only been back in Bellbrook since last year and didn't realize how much I missed it. I'm not ready to leave again."

"I wouldn't leave either if I were you," Saskia said

as they walked toward the stairs. "Let me give you some advice. Don't tell my dad yet. When he hears the word *no* he takes it as a challenge."

Is it possible that Leila said no to Damien? Did he make her an offer, then kill her when she said no?

"He'll assume you're trying to negotiate a better deal," Saskia continued, interrupting Karla's internal dialogue. "My dad thinks everything and everyone is negotiable. He loves the chase, and his perseverance will drive you nuts. Tell him you're thinking about it, then don't tell him your answer until we're about to lift anchor and sail away. It'll be easier for you."

If I decline Damien's offer, could I end up like Leila?

SIXTEEN

ALIBIS AND BOWLING ALLEYS

"LA-LA!" Max jogged down the hall to catch up. "Dad said you were here! How's dinner?"

"Probably cold by now," Karla replied. "But it was delicious until I left."

"Why did you leave?" Max asked.

Karla tugged Max's sleeve and led her to a quiet corner. Speaking in hushed tones, she told her sister about Damien's job offer, Caitlin's less than enthusiastic reaction, Saskia running away, her search for the missing social media star, and their conversation on the lower deck.

"You've been as busy as Dad and me," Max commented.

"What have you and Dad found out?"

"We went through the suitcase you found hidden on the boat."

"Tell me!" Karla whisper-yelled.

"We found Leila' purse. The killer crammed the brown leather satchel inside the suitcase."

"That's all of Leila's luggage accounted for, right?" Karla asked.

Max nodded. "We also found a burner phone with the same phone number Leila used to check into The Seascape Hotel," Max began. "It was only ever used to call and text one number."

"Whose?" Karla asked.

"We don't know." Max shook her head and rolled her eyes. "The number she was communicating with seems to be another burner phone. But their texts were pretty spicy." She wiggled her eyebrows. "No photos though. Just text messages."

"I bet she used that phone to communicate with her boyfriend," Karla hypothesized.

"That's what we think too," Max concurred. "Dad's getting the cyber cop to trace the burner phone. Hopefully he'll find out where and when she bought it."

"Did you find her ID?" Karla asked. "Did you find out where she lived? Can you contact her family?"

"That's the weird part," Max revealed. "The contents of Leila's satchel contained the usual stuff you'd expect. Portable phone charger, hand sanitizer, make-up, a couple of random pens, granola bars, and her wallet. But the wallet was empty. No driver's license, no credit cards, no bank cards. Nothing with Leila's name or photo. There was no ID in her suitcase either. But she must've had a passport because she told the hotel clerk she flew here."

"Do you think the killer kept her ID?" Karla asked. "Like a twisted trophy or something?"

"I don't know what to think," Max admitted. "But Dad says he might have to call in the feds."

"The feds?!"

"Shhh," Max hushed, looking over her shoulders to make sure they were still alone.

"Why the feds?"

"He suspects Leila might have been some kind of operative," Max revealed in a voice so quiet that Karla had to move her ear closer to her sister's mouth. "Damien Casey's political connections, Leila's missing ID, the lack of tags on her clothes, that she lied to access the yacht, and he thinks the spicy texts between Leila and her mystery boyfriend could be some kind of code."

"Code?"

"He thinks they could be instructions to Leila from her handler but disguised as intimate messages. Dad thinks it's possible that someone sent Leila here to spy on Damien, or worse."

"He suspects Leila came here to *kill Damien?*" Karla mouthed the last two words. "But that wouldn't make sense. Why would a covert operative travel with so much luggage? And don't people like that usually blend into their surroundings? Leila had tattoos, trendy hair, and fluorescent pink luggage." She shook her head.

"No, I don't believe anyone sent Leila here to assassinate Damien."

"We can't rule it out," Max said. "Damien Casey has just as many political enemies as he does friends."

"If Dad calls in the feds, I'm screwed," Karla whispered, her heart pounding against her ribs like it was trying to escape. "You've heard him complain about how slow and inefficient federal investigators are. The feds will take forever to solve Leila's murder. Rumours that Saskia and Ben are involved in a murder investigation are already threatening the wedding. If the feds show up, it'll confirm the rumours." She squeezed Max's hand. "I need this wedding, Max. I've invested everything I have into renovating and restoring Bellcroft. Half the businesses in town are relying on me to make it a successful event venue again. Saskia's wedding will either make or break me."

"I don't want the feds sniffing around either," Max admitted. "Dad says they'd only help. Act as consultants. But we all know they'll use their authority to take over the case. I'll talk to Dad and try to stall him," she offered. "I'll tell him you're still talking to the witnesses and getting new information and remind him that if he calls in the feds to 'help'"—she put air quotes around *help*—"they won't let you, a civilian, anywhere near the investigation, and we'll lose your insight."

"I should get back to the upper deck," Karla said, checking the time on her phone. "The others will wonder where I got to."

"One more thing," Max said in her normal voice before going back into whisper mode, "we reviewed the footage from the cameras outside Damien and Caitlin's offices. Saskia never entered Damien's office yesterday. Damien lied. He wasn't in his office all morning, either. He left with plenty of time to kill Leila. Same for Caitlin. She was alone in her office for a brief time before she went into town, but after she returned to the yacht with Leila, she never went back to her office. Since there are no other cameras covering the inside of the yacht…"

"No one has an alibi," Karla said, finishing Max's sentence. "Saskia admits she was alone in her cabin, Ben and Damien both lied about being with her, and Caitlin lied about being in her office." Karla sighed and dropped her shoulders in defeat. "Any of them could be the killer."

"Or all of them," Max pointed out. "Or some of them. We can't rule out anyone who was on the yacht from the time Leila arrived until you found her floating in the tub."

"I'll text you and Dad if I discover anything else," Karla said.

"Me too," Max agreed. "I'm going to interview the crew again tonight. Maybe you could observe the interviews and let me know if you pick up on any lies?"

"Of course," Karla said. "I'll do anything to help solve this mystery and get Saskia's wedding back on track."

They agreed Max would text Karla when she was ready to begin the second round of interviews.

"THERE YOU ARE!"

Karla was about to climb the stairs to the upper deck when Damien approached her from behind.

"Here I am." She smiled.

"We thought you got lost," he said in his slow, southern cadence.

"I'm not lost," Karla assured him. "Just distracted. I ran into my sister after I spoke with Saskia."

"We thought maybe you were giving yourself a tour of your future home," Damien retorted with a grin. "I'd be happy to show you around The Aquaholic. Wait till you see our media room and on-board gym. We even have a bowling alley—"

"I appreciate the generous offer, Damien," Karla said, interrupting his sales pitch, "but I'll need some time to think about it. I don't make life-changing decisions quickly."

"Of course," Damien responded. "Take all the time you need. If there's anything I can say or do to help you decide, let me know." His hand hovered so close to the small of Karla's back that she could feel heat radiate from it as he guided her away from the stairs. "How was your conversation with Saskia?" he asked quietly.

"I've been worried about her non-stop since that dead woman turned up in the bathtub."

"She's coping," Karla replied, not wanting to breach Saskia's privacy by recounting their entire discussion. "Yesterday shook her up, but she seems more distressed about the sponsors' threats to back out of the wedding."

"She doesn't need sponsors," Damien declared with a muffled snort. "If they back out, I'll make sure Saskia still has the wedding of her dreams."

"She might not *need* sponsors, Damien, but she *wants* them. It's important to her."

"What can I do?" he asked. "How can I fix this for my daughter?"

Karla told Damien about her plan to reach out to the sponsors and convince them to wait a while longer before abandoning Saskia and Ben's wedding. Then she told him about her plan to help the police solve the murder before Dean had to call in the feds to help.

"I agree with you and Max." Damien nodded. "The last thing we need is a bunch of federal agents sticking their noses where they don't belong. Using their authority to sniff around The Aquaholic and my business."

"That's why I've agreed to help them," Karla said. "Max is planning to re-interview the crew tonight. She asked me to observe and let her know if I detect any lies."

"Someone on this yacht must know more than

they're letting on about Leila," Damien agreed. "Karla, you have my full support and permission to access anything you need to help solve this murder."

"Thank you, Damien," Karla said. "Since I'm needed here for the interviews, I've arranged for Lynn, my mother and assistant, to meet you at Bellcroft for the night tour. Saskia said she was fine with it. I made sure Gucci won't be there, so Ben can relax and enjoy the tour this time."

"That's fine with me," Damien said. "Let me know what else I can do to help move this investigation along."

"It would be helpful if you told the truth about where you were yesterday between leaving your office and greeting me on the upper deck."

"I told you that I was working in my office all morning." He did not tilt his head and look at Karla from the side of his face, but he adjusted the always-present unlit cigar in his shirt pocket. She wondered if he was consciously forcing himself to abandon his old Tell, now that it was public knowledge, and was unconsciously replacing it with a new one.

"Except you weren't," she challenged. "The police reviewed the footage from the camera outside your office. You left mid-morning and didn't return all day. You had plenty of time to kill Leila."

"I did not kill that woman," Damien protested. "I didn't kill anyone."

"Then tell the truth about where you were so the

police can verify your alibi and eliminate you as a suspect. The more suspects they can eliminate, the faster they'll figure out who the killer is."

"Fine." Damien sucked in a long breath and blew it out. "I was at the gym for about an hour and a half. Usually, I go first thing in the morning, but yesterday a few early overseas calls disrupted my routine, so I went later. I use one of those interactive exercise bikes. It has a computer screen, and I can summon a live trainer whenever I want. The computer keeps track of my progress and workout statistics. The police will be able to verify that I was there and even speak to the trainer. After that, I had a shower in my cabin and ordered lunch from the kitchen. I had an open-faced chicken sandwich smothered in gravy. You can ask the chef. He took my order. You can also ask the deckhand who delivered it."

Without an exact timeline of his morning, it was impossible for Karla to determine whether Damien would have had the time to squeeze in a murder between the gym, his shower, and lunch. That would be a puzzle for Max and Dean to figure out.

"Why did you lie to the police?" Karla demanded.

"Because according to my daughter, whom I love dearly, her fiancé was in the gym all morning."

"Good!" Karla declared. "You and Ben can verify each other's alibis."

"Except we can't."

After a moment of confusion, Karla realized what Damien wasn't saying.

"Ben wasn't at the gym, was he?"

Damien shook his head.

If Ben wasn't with Saskia, and he wasn't at the gym when Leila was murdered, where was he?

SEVENTEEN

HERE, THERE, AND EVERYWHERE

"IF I ADMIT I was at the gym but didn't see Ben there, it will essentially point the finger of suspicion at my future son-in-law and break my daughter's heart at the same time." Damien shook his head. "I will not break my daughter's heart, Karla."

"Would you rather she married a potential murderer?" Karla whispered.

"Ben Underwood is not a murderer." Damien laughed at the notion. "He doesn't have the gumption."

"What does that mean?" Karla asked, frustrated that Damien wasn't taking Ben's status as a murder suspect seriously.

"Ben isn't capable of murder." Damien chuckled. "A few weeks ago, he refused to get out of the car because there was a puppy on the sidewalk. Twenty feet away. It was on a leash." He shook his head. "That boy sat in the car for fifteen minutes, shaking like a shirt in a hurricane until the puppy's owner moved along. It was a small dog, Karla." Damien pinched his thumb and index finger together until there was just a sliver of space between them. "Tiny."

"Do you like Ben?" Karla asked, crossing her hands in front of her chest and locking eyes with her client. "Do you want him and Saskia to get married?"

Damien reached for his unlit cigar, twirled it in his pocket twice, then stopped.

Was he about to lie but chose to tell the truth instead?

"Ben wouldn't have been my first choice for Saskia," Damien admitted. "In my opinion, she needs a strong partner. Someone with enough fortitude to challenge her impulsivity and not give in to every single demand she makes."

It was not lost on Karla that Damien was guilty of the same traits he found lacking in Ben. As far as Karla could tell, Damien didn't challenge his daughter's spontaneous tendencies and gave her whatever she wanted, whenever she wanted it.

"Ben might not be my first choice for son-in-law," Damien continued, "but Saskia loves him, so I've welcomed him into the family with open arms." He pulled the unlit cigar from his shirt pocket and slid it under his nose, sniffing it. "If Ben Underwood is a murderer, I'll eat my cigar." He clenched the stogie between his teeth as he grinned.

"Well, isn't this cozy?" Caitlin's voice oozed

sarcasm. "We were wondering where you two had disappeared to." She closed the distance between them and scanned Karla and Damien from head to toe, then back again. "We're waiting for you so we can have dessert. Chef made bruléed cardamom cheesecake topped with pistachio bark and candied kiwi slices."

"Sounds wonderful," Damien said, rubbing his tummy. "We should head upstairs and enjoy it."

Karla's phone dinged. "I have to run," she said, checking the screen.

MAX:

About to interview the crew. Meet me on the quarterdeck.

"What a shame," Caitlin said with less sincerity than a wet rag. "We'll be sure to save you a piece." She plastered a fake smile on her face.

Karla replied to Max's text with a thumbs-up emoji and slid the phone into her pocket.

"Go!" Damien encouraged. "The faster we solve this, the better."

"I MIGHT BE the captain of this ship, but I'm not the boss," Captain Peterson claimed in his Aussie accent. "I work for Mr. Casey. He signs my very generous pay cheque, and in exchange, I do what he says."

"Were you aware that certain security protocols, like

the tender logs, were not strictly adhered to?" Max asked, scribbling in her notebook.

"We've become more lax with the logs recently," he admitted.

"Was everyone lax? Or just certain crew members?"

"Whoever drives the tender logs arrivals and departures," Captain Peterson explained. "Since several of us take turns driving, I suppose it's fair to say that we've all been lax." He fiddled with his thick wedding band, slipping it up his finger, over his middle knuckle, spinning it, then sliding it back into place.

Karla found the shiny object distracting and had trouble focussing on the conversation when he fidgeted with it. *Stupid ADHD*, she thought. The ring was a fusion of deco and industrial design. It was wide, spanning the entire distance between Captain Peterson's bottom and middle knuckles. It was gold, and the hammered texture created dozens of tiny dimples that reflected the light.

"Is driving the tender a scheduled task?" Max continued her line of questioning. "Are crew members assigned specific days and times that they drive people to and from The Aquaholic?"

"No," Captain Peterson replied. "It's decided on an ad hoc basis. I assign whichever crew member is available when someone needs to be dropped off or picked up." He shrugged one shoulder. "If no one is available, I'll do it. Mr. Casey and Ben are both experienced boaters. It's not uncommon for them to drive themselves to shore and moor the boat until they drive it back."

There was a pause in the conversation while Max brought her notes up-to-date.

Captain Peterson waited, spinning his wedding ring and bouncing his knee.

"We're being more diligent with the logs now," he added, filling the silence. "Earlier today, I met with the crew and reiterated the importance of maintaining thorough records of everyone who boards and leaves The Aquaholic. It's important to me, and to Mr. Casey, that everyone on board feels safe."

"Did anyone tell you they felt unsafe?" Max asked, looking up from her notebook to meet Captain Peterson's gaze.

He shook his head.

"Do you feel unsafe?"

"I didn't," he said slowly, seeming to choose his words carefully. "But I admit, finding the dead woman in the guest cabin left me shaken." He shifted awkwardly in his seat and crossed his ankles, bringing an end to his knee bouncing. "I figured if I was anxious, then others probably are too."

More silence while Max made notes.

"Why are you here?" Captain Peterson asked, looking at Karla.

"She's helping us with our inquiries," Max replied on Karla's behalf without looking up from her notebook.

"I met your mother earlier," he said, smiling at Karla. "Lynn, I believe she's called?"

"That's right," Karla said, nodding. "She mentioned running into you outside Déjà Brew."

"The resemblance is remarkable," he commented. "I stopped her because I thought she was you. When I realized she wasn't, I asked her if she was your sister."

"They get that a lot," Max muttered.

"Lynn was really helpful," Captain Peterson continued. "I only wanted directions to a florist, but she insisted on taking the information and ordering the flowers for me." He smiled and unlocked his phone, tapping the screen a few times, then turning it toward Karla and holding it out so she could see it. "My wife received them about an hour ago. She loved them. Lynn did great. Be sure to thank her again for me, will you?"

"Of course," Karla said. "It's a beautiful arrangement. I'm glad your wife liked them."

"It's not the same as being there in person, but at least she knows I'm thinking about her." He gave the photo one final, wistful smile, then locked his phone, and placed it on his lap.

"Does your job keep you away from home a lot?" Karla asked.

"For months at a time," Captain Peterson replied. "Sometimes I get quite homesick. I miss my wife, our dogs, and my garden. Gardening is a horrible choice of hobby when you spend most of the year in the middle of the ocean." He smiled and his gaze drifted away.

"Mr. Casey is great, though. He pays to fly her here, or he'll hire a freelance captain to fill in so I can go home for a visit. We'd love to see each other more often, but her career keeps her anchored to our hometown." His half-hearted smile told Karla that Captain Peterson missed his wife and wasn't thrilled with their separate living arrangements.

He slid his wedding band up and down his finger again.

"Your ring is lovely," Karla complimented. "I've never seen one like it. It's so unique."

"Thank you." Captain Peterson slipped off the ring and pinched it between his thumb and forefinger. "It was custom made. My wife and I designed it together." He performed an impressive steeplechase flourish, rolling the metal band across the backs of his tanned fingers from his index to his pinky, and back again. "I never take it off. Ever." He let out a half laugh. "Except when I fidget with it. But it's always with me."

Karla couldn't take her eyes off the thing but also couldn't figure out why she was so mesmerized by it.

"Mr. Casey is a great employer. He takes great care of his employees," Captain Peterson continued, pointing his chin at Karla. "I hear you might join us on board permanently."

"Where did you hear that?" Karla asked. "I only found out a couple of hours ago."

"Caitlin mentioned it when she came up here earlier to schedule a tender to take Mr. Casey, her, Saskia, and

Ben ashore to tour the wedding venue after dinner this evening."

"Damien sounds like a generous employer," Karla said, steering the conversation back to Captain Peterson's employer. "You're the second person who has mentioned that he often pays to fly family and friends to visit. No matter where you are in the world."

"Who else mentioned it?" he asked.

"Caitlin was telling us yesterday that Damien flies her sister, niece, and nephew to visit the yacht," Max replied.

"Not only that," Karla added, "but he helps look after the kids so Caitlin and her sister can spend time together."

"He used to," Captain Peterson responded. "Damien used to fly them out quite often, but it's been at least two years since Caitlin's had an onboard visit from anyone."

More proof that Caitlin lied about her relationship with her sister. But why? Was she trying to make Damien look good? To make it seem like such a generous employer couldn't possibly be a murderer? That someone who entertains kids so their employees can have a break would never kill someone?

"Who do you think killed Leila?" Max asked out of nowhere.

"Not anyone aboard The Aquaholic," replied the captain without hesitation. "If Leila could sneak aboard the vessel, someone else could too."

"Where were you yesterday between returning to The Aquaholic from your morning coffee run and discovering Leila's body?" Max asked, her gaze boring into the captain.

"I was here, there, and everywhere." Captain Peterson gestured vaguely around him. "I spent most of my time on the quarterdeck. But I also met with the chef briefly, spoke with a few crew members, ran into Mr. Casey and spent a few minutes discussing logistics." He shook his head. "I keep telling Mr. Casey that we need onboard surveillance cameras. Not in the private areas, but in the communal areas. If he'd listened to me and installed them, I'd be able to prove where everyone was, wouldn't I?"

Karla and Max couldn't argue with that logic.

"Did Mr. Casey explain why he's hesitant to install surveillance cameras?"

"He's fussy about his privacy, and he worries his adversaries could hack into them." Captain Peterson replied. "He swears it's not because he has anything to hide."

If he has nothing to hide, why was Damien so against installing cameras for his and his family's safety?

EIGHTEEN

THE BARKING LOT

TWO DAYS after the murder

"An extra large?" Karla's eyes lit up at the sight of the huge to-go cup with the Déjà Brew logo emblazoned on the side. "Either you're an angel in lilac scrubs, or you somehow knew I didn't sleep last night." She smiled.

"The extra-large is my way of apologizing," Rob said, handing Karla the vanilla cold brew of iced coffee. "I'm sorry I didn't phone you yesterday after the autopsy. When Leila died, I had to switch from family-physician-mode to coroner-mode and reschedule a bunch of patients. I tried to see as many of them as I could yesterday after I finished the autopsy. By the time I got home, it was late, and I was exhausted. Then I video-called Josie at her dad's house to talk about her day and say goodnight. After that, I fell asleep until an hour ago."

"You have nothing to apologize for," Karla insisted, cracking the lid on her coffee and savouring the caffeinated aroma. "Bellbrook is lucky to have such a dedicated doctor. Josie is lucky to have such an awesome mother, and I'm lucky to have such an amazing best friend."

"Where's Gucci?" Rob asked, using her hand as an impromptu visor to block the early morning sun as she scanned The Barking Lot, Bellbrook's dog park, for the fast terrier. "There he is!" Her finger followed the speedy pup as he zoomed past them in pursuit of a black and white border collie.

They stood in comfortable silence, watching the border collie's owner throw a frisbee. The border collie took off in pursuit of the flying disc, and Gucci took off in pursuit of the border collie.

"This will tire him out," Rob said, smiling at the rushing dogs.

"Nothing tires him out. He's made of perpetual energy," Karla responded, then savoured the refreshing first mouthful of caffeine as it coated her throat and stomach.

They wandered to the fenced perimeter of the dog park.

"So... why didn't you sleep last night?" Rob asked, examining Karla's face with that I'm-a-trained-medical-professional look in her eyes.

"Couldn't stop thinking about Leila's murder,"

Karla admitted. "We have a ship full of suspects and can't eliminate any of them." She sipped her iced coffee. "On the upside, Saskia's wedding sponsors have agreed to give the police forty-eight hours to solve the murder and clear Saskia and Ben's names. After that, they're pulling their sponsorships."

"So, you have a forty-eight-hour deadline to save the biggest wedding in Bellbrook history," Rob paraphrased.

Karla nodded.

"If anyone can do it, you, Max, and Dean can."

"I wish I had your confidence," Karla commented between sips.

"I have enough confidence for both of us," Rob said as they sat on a nearby bench shaded by an old maple tree. "I also have a theory about how Leila died. She did not die by drowning." Rob leaned in and lowered her voice. "She was already dead when the killer submerged her in water. And I found more fibres in her throat and lungs. The fibres matched one of the pillows on the bed. Combine that with the hairs we found on the bed that matched Leila's hair, and in my opinion, Leila's killer smothered her on the bed."

"So, we're looking for someone strong enough to move her from the bed to the bathtub," Karla surmised.

"Leila was a petite woman," Rob added. "It wouldn't have been too difficult for most adults to move her such a short distance. I can't tell if the killer carried or dragged her from the bed to the tub. But Dean and Max think the killer was inside the cabin for quite a while. If the killer had enough time to move the body and remove some of her luggage, they would've had enough time to drag her to the bathtub."

"I think the killer put Leila in the empty tub, then filled it with water," Karla theorized. "There was a small puddle of water near the tub when we found her." She recalled how the sunlight streaming through the window had made the wet floor glisten. "But not as much water as you'd expect from dropping a hundred pounds of dead weight into a partially filled tub."

"That makes sense. Also, the killer probably would have been soaking wet if they'd placed the body in a full tub of water. It would have been harder for them to move around the yacht undetected if they were drenched," Rob agreed, pulling her foot onto the bench and turning her body to face Karla. "It could've happened like this"—she handed her coffee to Karla— "Leila and the killer had an altercation. The killer pushed her onto the bed and suffocated her with a pillow." Rob held her hands in front of her like she was smothering an invisible person with an invisible cushion. Her long, ginger ponytail shook as she applied pressure to the pretend pillow. "When the killer realized Leila was dead, they panicked. For whatever reason, possibly believing that the bath water would wash away evidence of the crime and create the illusion that Leila's death was accidental, the killer carried or dragged Leila to the bathtub, plugged the drain, and turned on the water."

"I see where you're going," Karla said, nodding. "While the tub filled with water, the killer tidied the bed and the cabin to conceal evidence of their struggle, went through Leila's stuff, and removed her ID to slow down the investigation... or because they're psychologically twisted and wanted a souvenir."

"By the time the killer returned to the tub to turn off the water, it was starting to overflow and some of it had sloshed onto the floor," Rob added.

"The killer turned off the water, closed the washroom door, and left the cabin with one of Leila's suitcases after cramming her purse inside," Karla continued. "Somehow, they transferred the luggage from the cabin where Leila died to the boat tender." She bit her lip, deep in thought. "There are lots of maintenance carts and food carts on the yacht," she continued. "The killer could have used a cart to move the luggage and covered it with a blanket or something."

"They probably would have moved the other suitcase too, and disposed of all the luggage, except you found the body and called the police before they had a chance," Rob concluded.

"Where's Leila's ID?" Karla wondered aloud. "It wasn't on the yacht or with the rest of Leila's belongings."

"The police missed the suitcase and purse the first

time they searched," Rob reminded her, then sipped her coffee. "Maybe they missed her ID, too. The killer seems to know the ship well. They knew how to get the luggage from the cabin to the tender without raising suspicion and had access to everything they needed to attempt to conceal their crime." She looked at Karla. "It was the perfect way to hide the missing luggage," Rob said. "The tender was so busy ferrying police and investigative equipment back and forth that it was never searched. Police officers literally sat on the missing luggage while complaining they couldn't find it." She shook her head. "I bet the killer laughed the entire time."

"You're right. Leila's killer hid her luggage in plain sight. A brazen move by the murderer," Karla agreed. "Everyone would have assumed the tender was searched and cleared since the police were using it." She swirled the remaining coffee in her cup.

"Do we think the killer did it on purpose?" Rob asked. "Did they make sure the police took the yacht tender with the luggage so it would have a better chance of being overlooked during the search?"

"But it was Damien who insisted on giving the police full access to the yacht tender to help with the investigation. Dad and Max were impressed with how generous and cooperative Damien was." Karla froze. "But if your theory is right, that would mean Damien hid the luggage, which would mean Damien killed

Leila." Her throat tightened, and something curdled in her stomach.

Rob said nothing, raising her eyebrows and gulping the rest of her iced coffee.

NINETEEN

CYNOPHOBIA

"OOH, look at that gorgeous set of wheels," Rob said as they left The Barking Lot and made their way toward Rob's car. "It's my dream car, and it's even my favourite colour." She gestured to the royal-blue Maserati in the parking lot outside the dog park.

Karla was crouched down, holding Gucci's portable water bottle while he took a drink. She looked over at the blue sports car just as someone with a distinct, trendy frohawk slid down the driver's seat until their head disappeared below the steering wheel.

"I think that's Ben Underwood," Karla said, squinting at the luxury car.

"The same Ben who's engaged to Saskia?" Rob asked. "I haven't met him."

"He's a nice guy, but his alibi is so fishy it should come with a side of chips and tartar sauce." Karla explained how Damien disproved Ben's alibi by admitting he had been at the gym the morning Leila was killed but didn't see Ben there.

"Did anyone on the yacht tell the truth about their alibi?" Rob asked.

"Why is Ben here, and where did he get a car?" Oblivious to Rob's question, Karla tugged Gucci's leash and changed direction, walking toward the Maserati. "The Barking Lot is a strange destination for someone who's terrified of dogs," she mumbled to herself.

"Why is he hiding from us?" Rob asked, jogging to catch up to her determined friend and dog. "He slid down as soon as we saw each other."

"He might not be hiding from *us*," Karla explained, coming to a stop a few spots away from the shiny blue sports car. "I think he's hiding from Gucci. Ben is terrified of dogs. He might've panicked when he saw Gucci getting closer."

"Gucci's small, and he's on a leash," Rob pointed out, skeptical. "Ben is inside a car. Gucci can't get to him."

"I know, but phobias aren't always logical." Karla extended her hand with the leash handle toward Rob. "Would you mind? Ben might not talk to me or even roll down the window if Gooch is nearby."

"Sure," Rob said, shrugging and taking the leash. "I have to get to work. I'll drop Gucci off at your place on the way."

"Thanks," Karla smiled. As Rob walked away, she shouted, "Gucci and I appreciate it. Oh, don't forget—"

"I know," Rob called back. "Fill his bowl with fresh water and three ice cubes."

"Thank you!" Karla waved, smiling.

Karla waited until Rob and Gucci were inside her car and out of sight. Then she approached the blue car and rapped her knuckles on the driver's side window.

Ben slid up into a seated position. He strained his neck, pressed his nose against the window, and searched the pavement around Karla's feet.

"He's. Not. Here," Karla emphasized each word so Ben could read her lips. "Gucci's not here," she said, shaking her head and waving her hands in a cancellation gesture, hoping he'd understand.

Ben inched the window open. "Where is he?" His voice was cautious.

"My friend took him home," Karla replied.

Ben opened the window the rest of the way.

"Nice car," Karla commented.

"Thanks." Ben stroked the top of the steering wheel. "It's a rental. Caitlin arranged it."

"What brings you to the dog park, Ben? Are you lost?"

"No," Ben replied, then sucked in a long breath. "I'm here on purpose." He exhaled slowly, closing his eyes and counting to four under his breath, then took in another big lungful of air.

"Are you doing a breathing exercise?" Karla asked.

Ben nodded during his slow exhale and wiped his palms on the thighs of his navy-blue sports shorts.

"Are you OK?"

"I think so," he said with the same cautious voice he used to ask where Gucci was.

"Should I phone Saskia?"

"No!" Ben's voice was loud, and his eyes were wide. "Please don't tell Saskia you saw me. She thinks I'm somewhere else."

"So, lying to your fiancé about your whereabouts is part of your normal routine?" Karla crossed her arms in front of her chest, tilted her head, and arched her brows.

"No, of course not," Ben retorted defensively. "Why would you think that?"

"Well, you lied to her about your whereabouts when Leila was killed, and you lied again today." She uncrossed her arms and forced her face and shoulders to relax. "What's going on Ben?"

"It's called exposure therapy," Ben replied. "It's part of my surprise wedding gift for Saskia. I'm getting help for my cynophobia."

"Sign-o-phobia?" Karla asked, trying out the new-to-her word.

"It means I have a phobia of dogs," Ben explained. "I'm getting help so I can surprise Saskia on our wedding day with a puppy. She's always wanted a dog."

"I see," Karla said. "And part of your exposure therapy is visiting the dog park?"

"Yes," Ben replied. "First, we—my therapist and I—talked about dogs. Then we looked at pictures of dogs.

Next, we watched videos of dogs. Now, I'm observing them in person. Soon, I'll graduate to being in the presence of a leashed dog, and eventually, I should be able to handle myself around an unleashed one. My therapist says that exposing myself to dogs in a safe, controlled environment will help me break the patterns of fear and avoidance I've been relying on since I was little. She says each exposure will decrease my overall anxiety, and I'll get used to being around dogs."

"Wow, Ben." Karla brought her hand to her heart. "This might be the sweetest, most thoughtful gift ever. Saskia will be so touched and happy."

"I hope so," replied the former football player. "It would be awful if I spent months torturing myself for nothing."

"It won't be for nothing," Karla assured him. "Just yesterday, Saskia mentioned that she's always wanted a dog. You're going through so much to make her dream come true."

Surely someone this thoughtful and selfless couldn't be a murderer.

"It's hard." Ben's shoulders slumped, his frown weighing down his face. "I hope I can do it. It's the most difficult thing I've ever done. I don't want Saskia to find out because, if I fail at this exposure therapy thing, it'll devastate her."

"You're doing great," Karla reassured him. "Yesterday at Bellcroft, you got out of the car while Gucci was on a leash. You walked past him. That's huge. I heard that a few weeks ago you couldn't even get out of the car because there was a dog on the sidewalk. You've made significant progress."

"Yeah, that's what my therapist said too." He didn't sound convinced.

"Is this where you were the morning Leila was killed?" Karla asked. "Were you at the dog park practising your exposure therapy? This car is a real eye-catcher. Someone would have noticed if you were here. The police can verify—"

Ben shook his head. "I wasn't here," he said. "This is my first visit to the dog park. The morning Leila died I was on the yacht. I can prove it."

"How?"

"Get in and I'll show you." Ben unlocked the car and patted the black leather passenger seat.

Karla moved toward the passenger side of the car, then hesitated. With the utmost discretion, she used her phone to snap a pic of the Maserati's rear license plate and sent it to Rob with a quick text message.

KARLA

Getting into this car with Ben. Also, I've shared my location with you, just in case.

With some of her anxious hesitation relieved, Karla continued around the car and climbed into the passenger seat.

"Where are we going?" she asked as Ben backed out of the parking spot.

"Do you want me to prove I didn't kill Leila?" he asked, narrowing his eyes on the road.

Answering a question with a question was Ben's Tell. He preferred to avoid lying by avoiding the question or changing the subject. Was he merely answering her question with a question, or was he avoiding lying to her because he didn't want her to know where he was taking her? What if this was a setup, and Ben's true motivation for visiting The Barking Lot was to lure Karla into this fancy car, so he could kill her and prevent her from exposing him as a murderer?

Did I just lock myself in a car with a killer?

TWENTY

ANKLES ARE TRICKY

BEN PULLED into a parking spot at the marina.

The drive had been quiet. When Karla had tried to engage Ben in conversation, he muttered one-syllable responses and kept his stare laser-focussed on the road. He was exuding a level of intensity Karla had never sensed from him before, and it made her nervous.

"Are we going to The Aquaholic?" Karla asked, getting out of the low car. "Is someone coming to pick us up?"

To catch up to Ben, Karla jogged delicately in her sand-coloured, open-toe canvas wedge shoes. She stopped just short of the dock.

"Yes and no," Ben replied without breaking his stride toward the yacht tender. "Yes, we're going to The Aquaholic, and no, we aren't getting picked up." He was halfway down the dock already and moving like they were in a race. "I drove myself to shore. I'll drive us back."

"Oh," Karla said, hoping her voice wasn't as shaky as the rest of her. "OK."

Watching Ben approach the sleek speedboat, Karla recalled yesterday evening, when Captain Peterson mentioned that Damien and Ben sometimes drove the tenders themselves to get to and from the yacht. That meant it could have been Ben who hid Leila's luggage on the tender. Maybe he was planning to transport the rest of her luggage to the tender too, then drive himself out to sea, and dispose of it. But they thwarted his plan when they discovered Leila's body and called the police. What if that was his plan now? What if Ben was using his alibi to coax Karla onto the speedboat, so he could drive her out to sea and dispose of her? After all, it was Karla who had convinced Damien to admit that Ben had lied about his alibi. Maybe he planned to eliminate her before she found proof that he was Leila's killer.

"Are you coming?" Ben called from the boat.

"Be right there!" Karla smiled, terrified that if she got on the speedboat, she would never stand on Bellbrook's beautiful shore again.

Approaching the dock, and desperate to stall for time, Karla pretended to roll her ankle. She was careful to choreograph her fall in such a way that her above-the-knee, button-down, short-sleeved, chambray dress wouldn't expose anything it shouldn't.

"*Ooof.*" She landed on the pavement and let out a gasp loud enough to get Ben's attention.

"Are you OK?" Ben leapt off the boat and jogged down the dock toward her.

"I'm fine," Karla insisted. "I just need a minute." She cradled her uninjured foot and made unnecessary wincing faces as she carefully rotated the unharmed ankle joint.

"Should I call your doctor friend?" Ben asked, his brows squeezed together with worry.

"No," Karla said. "Rob is busy with patients today."

What should I do? Think, Karla, think! I know. I'll call Lynn to pick me up. That way, I can avoid getting on the tender without accusing him of anything.

"Ankles are tricky. I know football players who lost their careers because of ankle injuries."

"Good thing I'm not a running back," Karla quipped, hoping her joke referenced the right sport.

"I'll help you up and drive you to the hospital." Ben crouched and steadied himself, preparing to lift Karla off the ground.

Getting back in the car with Ben didn't seem like a much better idea than getting on the yacht tender with him. She was about to protest—as politely as possible—and whip out her phone to call Lynn.

"Oh good! You're still here!" Caitlin Lopez strode toward them with wide, fast strides.

Karla had never been so happy to see her.

"I thought I'd missed you and would have to call for

someone to pick me up." Caitlin looked down at Karla's contorted body on the ground. "What happened?"

"She twisted her ankle," Ben replied. "Since you can't drive the tender yourself, you'll have to call someone to pick you up, anyway. I'm going to drive Karla to the hospital."

Caitlin can't drive a speedboat? This would make her a less likely suspect, right? It wouldn't have made sense for her to hide Leila's luggage on the tender if she wasn't able to drive the tender somewhere to dispose of it.

"Oh no!" Either Caitlin's concern was genuine, or she was a better actor than Karla gave her credit for. "Let me help." She pressed her hands against her hips and assessed the situation. "I'll hold her ankle steady while you lift her."

Ben nodded.

"Wait!" Karla said, "I think I'm OK." She lifted her foot off the ground and rotated her ankle. "It's a bit stiff," she fibbed, staring at her shoe to avoid looking either of them in the eye, "but I don't think it's serious enough to warrant a trip to the hospital."

"Are you sure?" Ben asked. "Walking on an injured ankle can make it worse."

"I'm sure," Karla replied.

Ben extended his hand to help her off the ground.

She rose to her feet, keeping her weight on her "good" foot and straightening her dress and bag.

Ben offered his arm and suggested she try a couple of tentative steps.

Karla obliged, adding a subtle limp for effect.

"It already feels better," she insisted.

"Take it slow," Ben cautioned. "Rest and elevate as much as possible for the next few days."

"I will," Karla assured him.

"It doesn't appear to be swollen," Caitlin commented, bending to inspect the unscathed joint.

Caitlin looked different today. She had changed her look. Her short caramel bob was slicked back, she wore large hoop earrings, and her usually neutral makeup was more dramatic. She had a smokey eye and dark red lipstick. Instead of her usual power suit, she wore a teal one-piece, wide-legged jumpsuit with a suspender neckline, and a pair of brown Tory Burch sandals. Her toenails were painted a dark red that matched her lipstick.

"I was lucky. It could have been worse," Karla said. "It's possible I panicked and overreacted." She rolled her eyes and chuckled. "It's been ages since I've worn these shoes. These wedge heels are like walking on stilts."

"Why are you here?" Caitlin asked. "Are you visiting The Aquaholic because your dad is there?"

"My dad is on the yacht?"

Caitlin nodded.

This helped Karla relax. Caitlin's presence combined with the knowledge that Dean was nearby, and the realization that dozens of people milling around the marina have witnessed her with Ben—especially after making such a spectacle of herself with the fake fall—made her more comfortable with getting on the tender.

With Karla using Ben's arm for support, the trio walked slowly onto the deck and toward the speedboat.

By the time they reached the boat, Karla had abandoned her pretend limp, declared herself miraculously healed, thanked Ben and Caitlin for their concern and help, and apologized for making such a big deal out of a minor injury.

"Why is my dad on the yacht?" Karla asked as Ben steered the boat away from the dock.

"Chief Sheridan and a couple of his officers are confiscating Damien's favourite exercise bike," Caitlin explained. "Apparently, it's evidence. He and Damien were vague, but Damien gave Chief Sheridan permission to take the bike and seemed to understand why the police wanted it. I assumed you knew Chief Sheridan was there, and you were joining him."

"Actually, I asked Karla to accompany me back to the yacht," Ben said. "I need to show her something."

"Oh?" Caitlin's interest was piqued.

"She found out about our little secret." Ben smirked at Caitlin. "She's on to us."

"How did that happen?" Caitlin asked, miffed.

Karla tried to hide her panic as it occurred to her

that Ben and Caitlin's secret could be that they killed Leila together.

"She found me at the dog park," Ben replied. "She was there with Gucci and her doctor friend."

Karla turned her head back and forth between Ben and Caitlin like she was watching a tennis match, following along as they talked about her like she wasn't there. *What secret? Someone tell me!*

"I hope you'll keep it to yourself," Caitlin said to Karla. "Ben's doing great, but if for some reason he doesn't progress enough to surprise Saskia with a puppy on their wedding day, she would be shattered."

"Of course," Karla said, relieved their shared secret was Ben's exposure therapy and not Leila's murder. "I wouldn't want to ruin the surprise. If Ben can prove that he couldn't have killed Leila, we can ask the police to keep his alibi under wraps."

"Caitlin helped find my therapist," Ben announced.

"Ben's making such good progress, and speaks so highly of his therapist, that I'm considering booking an appointment with her to discuss my own issues." Caitlin smiled.

Karla couldn't tell if Caitlin was joking and wondered what issues she might want to discuss with a professional therapist. Her relationship with her sister? Her limerence with Damien? *It's none of my business,* Karla reminded herself. *Anyway, she was probably kidding.*

"I love your jumpsuit," Karla said, shifting the foot

she had elevated for appearance's sake so Caitlin could sit across from her.

"Thank you," Caitlin said, smiling and smoothing her wide pant leg. "I'm trying something different. Something a little more me." She nodded. "It's a nice change."

If she wasn't herself before, who was she?

They left the tender and boarded the yacht. Caitlin offered to accompany Ben for moral support. He thanked her and accepted her offer. Karla and Caitlin followed Ben to the same deck where Karla had found Saskia the previous evening after the social media maven had run from the dinner table in tears.

Ben led them to the same white deck box where Karla and Saskia had sat and talked less than twenty-four hours prior. Ben opened the large white box. Caitlin held the lid for him, even though the hinge locked in place when the box was open all the way. Ben rifled through the contents and came out with a black cinch bag. He closed the box, pulled open the cinch bag, and dumped its contents on the closed lid.

Karla watched as two stuffed dogs—a stuffed miniature schnauzer and a stuffed chocolate lab—a couple of picture books, a journal, and a pen tumbled onto the white box.

"What's this?" Karla asked, assuming it had something to do with Ben's exposure therapy, but not sure.

"This is where I was when that Leila woman was killed," Ben explained. "I told Saskia I was going to the gym, but I came here. I've been coming here three times per week to meet with my therapist."

"Online," Caitlin clarified. "Ben and his therapist have video appointments."

"I see," Karla said. She reached toward the objects on the deck box, then stopped herself. "May I?"

"Help yourself." Ben gestured toward the assortment of dog-themed items.

Karla picked up a book. *"Big Dogs, Little Dogs, A Visual Guide To Popular Breeds,"* she read aloud, then leafed through the picture book. She put it down and picked up the other book, Pop-Up Puppies. She opened it to a random page and a cardboard Irish Setter rose from the thick pages. She turned the page and a Jack Russell Terrier popped up in the middle of the two-page spread.

"My therapist can confirm I was here," Ben said. "We spent two hours together." He unlocked his phone. "I can show you the video we watched. It was a video of a dog park." He turned his phone toward Karla. "It helped prepare me for my trip to The Barking Lot today."

"I believe you," Karla said. "But you need to explain this to the police."

"They won't tell Saskia and spoil the surprise, will they?" he asked.

"I hope not," Karla replied. "They'll only mention it to her if they have no choice. The police aren't here to ruin your wedding gift to your future wife. They're here to solve a murder."

"Chief Sheridan is here," Caitlin reminded him. "You can use my office if you want to have a discreet word with him."

"Thanks, Caitlin." Ben smiled.

Karla texted Dean and asked him to meet them at Caitlin's office. She told him that Ben would like to clarify his alibi. Dean replied that he was on his way.

Rounding the corner to Caitlin's office, Karla's phone dinged.

"My car's ready," she announced. Ben and Caitlin looked at her, confused. "It's been in the shop for days," Karla explained. "It's finally ready, and I can stop relying on everyone I know to drive me around." She checked the time on her phone. "Ben, would you mind if I left to pick up my car? It'll take about an hour. The dealership is in Beaver Creek, the next town over."

"How will you get there without a car?" Caitlin asked.

"Lynn offered to take me," Karla replied.

"Why don't I take you?" Ben suggested. "The rental car is still at the marina. It'll give me an excuse to drive the Maserati again. It's a nice ride."

"I think you should talk to Chief Sheridan while Saskia is occupied," Caitlin advised. "She's giving a podcast interview right now, but when she's finished, she'll want to know where you are."

"Good point," Ben agreed.

"Why don't I drive Karla to pick up her car," Caitlin suggested, narrowing her eyes on Karla with one corner of her mouth curling into a crooked grin. "It'll give us a chance to talk." She looked at Ben. "As long as you're comfortable meeting with Chief Sheridan on your own, of course."

"I'll be fine," Ben assured her, then fished the Maserati keys from his pocket and tossed them to Caitlin who caught them with ease.

"Road trip." Caitlin smirked at Karla, dangling the fob between her thumb and forefinger.

TWENTY-ONE

LEAD-FOOT LOPEZ

CAITLIN DROVE CAREFULLY THROUGH TOWN, but as soon as they hit the open road, she put the pedal to the metal, leaving Bellbrook, posted speed limits, and her instinct for self-preservation behind them in the rear-view mirror. *Lead-foot Lopez,* Karla mentally nicknamed her.

The windows were down, and the wind roared in Karla's ears. She could practically feel the tangles and knots forming as her wavy blonde hair swirled and billowed in all directions around her head. She was a stark contrast to Caitlin's serene smile, relaxed face, and perfectly smooth hair; the wind hardly touched Caitlin's slicked back bob.

Caitlin pressed a button, and the windows closed.

Karla's hair settled, and she did her best to detangle and smooth her windblown tresses with her fingers.

"I'm glad we have this chance to talk," Caitlin

began. "I have some questions about your ability to detect lies."

"What do you want to know?"

"How long have you been able to tell when I'm"—there was an awkward pause while Caitlin chose her words—"not completely truthful?"

"The past few days," Karla replied. "After Leila's murder." She looked at Caitlin. "I don't *want* to know your Tell, it's just something that happens sometimes. In fact, most of the time I try to ignore people's Tells. I'm sorry if it makes you uncomfortable." She sighed. "This is why I don't disclose it to many people."

"I was in shock at first," Caitlin admitted. "But I'm fine with it now. I'm trying *very* hard to kick the habit." Caitlin chuckled.

This was the first time Karla had heard Caitlin crack a joke. Her hair and makeup weren't the only things that were different about Damien's executive assistant today. *This is going better than I expected,* Karla thought to herself. *I won't bother telling Caitlin she'll probably develop new Tells to replace the one she's become aware of.*

They laughed together. Caitlin laughing at her own joke, and Karla laughing with relief that Caitlin wasn't angry at her for revealing her Tell in front of Damien, which in hindsight she regretted, even though Caitlin had challenged her to disclose it.

"Have you figured out everyone else's Tell?" Caitlin asked. "Can you detect when Saskia or Ben are lying? What are their Tells?"

Karla was neither shocked nor offended that Caitlin was curious about other people's Tells. She had often wondered what she would do if she couldn't detect lies and met someone who could. She figured she would ask them to tell her other people's Tells, and maybe even ask them to teach her how to do it.

"I can't detect everyone's lies," Karla explained, without answering the question. "But the more time I spend with someone, the more likely I'll figure out their Tells. Some people use multiple Tells, which makes their lies harder to detect, and some people don't have Tells. Either I can't figure them out, they're brutally honest, or because they don't experience any stress when they lie."

"Can you teach me how to do it?" Caitlin asked, closing in on the red pickup truck ahead of them.

"I don't think so," Karla replied, watching the pickup truck in front of them grow larger as they sped close enough for her to read the bumper sticker that said, *If you can read this, you're too close.* "Rob suspects it's a combination of neurological and central nervous responses that result from my ADHD and probable SPS." Karla gripped the grab handle and swallowed hard, hoping Caitlin realized how fast they were approaching the pickup truck in front of them.

"So, it's like a symptom?" Finally, Caitlin turned on the indicator, pressed her foot onto the gas pedal and swerved left at the last possible moment, narrowly avoiding the pickup truck before easing back in front of it.

"More or less," Karla agreed, watching the pickup truck get smaller and smaller in the passenger-side mirror. She let out a silent sigh of relief. "It's not a skill I've cultivated or taught myself."

"Well, you've fascinated Damien with your unique skill," Caitlin said, her jaw tensing as she spoke. "He's obsessed with you."

"He's obsessed with the skill," Karla corrected, "and how it could benefit him."

"Are you planning to accept his job offer?" Caitlin tightened her grip on the steering wheel until her knuckles were white, and Karla could discern the shape of the bones underneath her skin.

"No."

Caitlin loosened her death grip on the steering wheel, and her jaw relaxed.

"You're relieved," Karla said, easing the conversation toward a topic she knew was taboo.

"Yes." Caitlin gave Karla a sideways glance from behind her sunglasses. "I guess there's no point in lying to you since you'll probably know, anyway."

"Lying is the best way to help me figure out your Tells," Karla cautioned.

"So, you've probably figured out that, in the past, I've lied to you about a few things."

"Yes," Karla nodded. "Why did you lie to Max and

me about your relationship with your sister and her kids?"

Caitlin sighed, and her shoulders slumped. "It's embarrassing," she admitted. "I allowed my career and my feelings for Damien to eclipse every other relationship in my life. I hardly ever saw my sister unless she came to visit me. Even then, I spent most of our time together working, talking about work, or distracted by work." Caitlin's voice grew thick with emotion as she spoke, then her voice hitched on the last two words. "I lost track of everything that was happening with the people I love. The last time I saw my niece and nephew, I couldn't remember what grades they were in or what activities they did outside of school. My sister's marriage fell apart, and I didn't even notice that she was heartbroken and struggling to cope."

She swiped her index finger under her eye behind her sunglasses and sniffled. "Our last conversation was a huge argument over the phone. My sister was fed up with our one-sided relationship. When she called me self-centred and told me I start every sentence with Damien's name, I hung up on her." Her voice was thick with regret and frustration. "I still can't believe I hung up on her. We haven't spoken or texted since."

"That's awful, Caitlin," Karla sympathized. "I hope you can mend your relationships with your family if that's what you want."

"I have lots of reasons for not wanting you to accept Damien's job offer, but the biggest one is that I would hate to watch someone else become so absorbed by Damien's world that they end up abandoning their life and their identity, like me."

"You feel you gave up your identity?" Karla asked.

"I gave up everything for him." Caitlin smacked the steering wheel, and the atmosphere in the car became tense. "I changed my hair, I changed the way I dress, I even changed the way I talk." She shook her head. "I did everything I could to become Damien's ideal woman. I paid attention to the women he dated and figured out what qualities attracted him. I studied them and transformed myself into his exact type." She shook her head and tears streamed down her cheeks from behind her sunglasses. "He should have noticed me. But he didn't, and I'm beginning to think he never will." She inhaled a sharp breath and pulled herself to her full seated height. "I'm tired of being invisible. I'm done. From now on I'm going back to me. The me *I'm* happy with. The *real* me."

"It must be exhausting pretending to be someone else," Karla commiserated. "You deserve someone who loves the real you. If this new look and new attitude are the real Caitlin Lopez, you're awesome. If Damien can't see that, it's his loss. There's someone out there who would love to be with the real you."

Karla believed every word she said to Caitlin, even if she didn't have enough personal experience with true love to back it up.

"Can I ask you a huge favour?" Caitlin asked.

"Would you ask Damien how he feels about me? Now that he knows you can tell when he's lying, he'll be more likely to tell the truth. And if he lies, you'll know. I just need to know if I have any chance with him, or if I've spent the past twenty years wasting my time."

"I can't do that, Caitlin," Karla replied. "Damien is my client. It would be unprofessional."

"I understand." Caitlin nodded, but her disappointment was palpable.

"Maybe you should ask Damien yourself," Karla suggested. "Trust your instincts. You'll know if he's being honest."

"I've tried to have that conversation with him so many times but always chicken out," Caitlin revealed. "I feel like it would open a door that could never close, you know?"

"I think so," Karla replied.

"Once I admit my feelings to him, I can't unsay it. Our working relationship would probably become awkward and unbearable. I'd probably want to leave, but leaving would mean giving up my job and my home." She sighed. "It's not like I have a life waiting for me outside of Damien and my job."

"I can give you a job," Karla blurted, without thinking through the potential ramifications of her statement. "You have all the qualities and experience to be a great concierge. Just Task Me! has concierges all over the world. You could choose your location. I can't provide housing or a multi-million-dollar mega yacht, but I'd hire you in a heartbeat." She paused. "Unless you turn out to be Leila's killer. In which case, I'd have to rescind the offer."

"I didn't kill Leila," Caitlin said. "Do you really think I'm capable of murder?"

"My dad says that, under the right circumstances, anyone could be capable of murder," Karla replied. "Everyone who was onboard The Aquaholic at the same time as Leila is a suspect. The police know you lied about your alibi. You claimed to be in your office all morning, but the surveillance camera aimed at your office door proved otherwise."

"I told the police I was working until you arrived," Caitlin clarified. "They assumed I was in my office. I never claimed to be there. I just didn't correct them because I didn't think it mattered where I was working."

"Where were you?"

"In my cabin," Caitlin replied. "I often work in my cabin."

"What were you working on?"

"I was rescheduling meetings," Caitlin replied. "A few days before we arrived in Bellbrook, Damien had asked me to clear his schedule so he could go with you, Saskia, and Ben to tour Bellcroft."

"We postponed the Bellcroft tour until the next day because we found Leila's body," Karla reminded her.

"The meeting Damien had that afternoon was originally scheduled for next week. I contacted the other party and moved the meeting forward so it would conflict with the Bellcroft tour. When we had to cancel the tour because of Leila's murder, I rescheduled again so it would conflict with the rescheduled tour the next day."

"Why would you do that?" Karla asked, confused.

"Because the people Damien was scheduled to meet with are horrible at time management. They cancel meetings at the last minute at least fifty percent of the time because they have a 'scheduling conflict'." When Caitlin took her hands off the wheel to put air quotes around 'scheduling conflict,' Karla's life flashed before her eyes. "I knew they would probably contact me to cancel just minutes before we were scheduled to video chat with them. I also knew that Damien wouldn't be suspicious because they regularly cancel at the last minute, even when we let them choose the date and time. I was right on both counts."

"You wanted them to cancel so you could be alone with Damien while Saskia, Ben, and I were away from the yacht," Karla surmised. *Saskia was right again! She's good!*

"I was going to have *The Talk* with him and tell him how I feel," Caitlin admitted. "But I lost my nerve at the last minute. I always lose my nerve at the last minute." She shifted in her seat and adjusted her grip on the steering wheel. "But not anymore. I'm going to get Damien alone and tell him how I feel."

"When?" asked Karla.

"As soon as the police arrest Leila's killer," Caitlin replied. "We're both too distracted right now." She glanced at Karla. "Text your father and your sister. Tell them to check my laptop. I'll give them my password. They can contact the people I spoke with the day Leila died and confirm my alibi. They can also get their tech people to confirm that I spent hours replying to emails and doing research for Damien."

Karla did as Caitlin instructed.

They drove in comfortable silence with Caitlin slowing down to about twenty over the speed limit; Karla was relieved when she spotted their exit.

Since last night, Karla had uncovered Damien's alibi—he was at the gym—Ben's alibi—he was on the smaller deck with his virtual therapist, getting desensitized to dogs—and Caitlin's alibi—she was in her cabin yearning for Damien and manipulating his schedule. Assuming these alibis were confirmable by the police, none of them could have killed Leila.

Most of the crew had been accounted for, apart from the deckhand who dropped off Leila's luggage, delivered a Cobb salad to her cabin, and served drinks on the upper deck just before they discovered Leila's body. Apparently, he was on a break, reading alone in his cabin.

The only non-crew member still unaccounted for was Saskia. She claimed to be alone in her cabin. Could Saskia be a killer? She had knowledge of the crime scene that she couldn't have seen firsthand, but she provided a reasonable explanation for how she learned that information. Over the past few days, Karla and Saskia had become friends, or so Karla had thought. Maybe the tears Saskia cried on the deck, and the bonding they did over their complicated relationships with their absent mothers was an act. Maybe Saskia was pretending to be Karla's friend so she could use Karla to find out what was happening with the police investigation. *If only I could tell when Saskia was lying,* Karla lamented to herself. Was she unable to figure out Saskia's Tell because there wasn't one? Was Saskia a sociopath, unburdened by a conscience and felt no remorse about lying... or even murder?

TWENTY-TWO

WATER CROWFOOT

"HOW'S YOUR CAR RUNNING?" Rob asked.

Karla, Rob, and Rosalie were sitting on the outdoor patio at Déjà Brew, sipping drinks, nibbling on treats, and watching the world go by.

"Purring like a kitten," Karla replied, sipping her iced tea and watching from the corner of her eye as Rosalie slipped a piece of lemon biscotti to Gucci under the table.

She gave Rosalie an accusatory stare.

"What?" the octogenarian asked, as though she had no clue what she had done. "It fell. I'm old. Sometimes my hands shake and stuff falls."

"Rosalie Howard, your hands are steadier than most surgeons," Rob chided.

Rosalie blushed. "Fine. I gave Gucci a tiny piece of biscotti. He's a good boy. He deserves a treat." Karla's phone chimed. "You should check that," Rosalie said, changing the subject. "It could be Lynn with an update about Harry."

Karla had stopped at home after she picked up her car to take Gucci for his afternoon walk. While she was there, Lynn called from her car. Apparently, Harry had sliced his hand with a rusty tool, or piece of gardening equipment, or something—it was difficult to hear with Lynn and Harry bickering and bantering while Lynn was also talking to Karla on the phone—and they were on their way to the hospital. Harry had been working outside Lynn's cottage when the accident happened. Thank goodness, Lynn was home. Alerted by Harry's loud string of curse words, she tended to his wound right away.

Harry insisted he was fine, but Lynn disagreed and convinced him to go to the hospital, certain he would need stitches and a tetanus shot. She asked Karla to pick up Rosalie and drive her to her weekly garden club meeting; something that Lynn did every week. So, Karla and Gucci picked up Rosalie and drove into town. They came early because Rosalie was craving a flat white and lemon biscotti from Déjà Brew. They ran into Rob at the cafe. She was taking a late lunch.

"It's Lynn," Karla confirmed. "Harry needed ten stitches and a tetanus shot. They're on their way back. Lynn says she's taking him home, feeding him, and getting him settled."

"I bet Harry's not happy," Rosalie said. "He likes to keep his hands busy. This injury will slow him down."

Karla nodded. "In Lynn's text, she said he was in a grumpy mood, complaining that he needed both hands to keep the grounds at Bellcroft in good shape."

"The Petal Pushers will help him out," Rosalie chimed in, offering the services of her gardening club. "Whether or not he likes it, I've already put our members on notice. The Petal Pushers love a gardening emergency." She sipped her coffee then said, "Remind me to take him a rhubarb-strawberry pie later."

"Did the physician prescribe him an antibiotic?" Rob asked.

"Lynn didn't say," Karla replied.

"Why did they go to the hospital?" Rob asked. "Lynn should have brought Harry to me for treatment."

"You're still getting caught up on your patient backlog from Leila's murder," Karla reminded her. "They didn't want to jump ahead of your appointments."

"I could've made time to give Harry a few stitches," Rob argued, somewhat insulted that Harry took his injured hand elsewhere.

"You can remove them," Rosalie suggested, appeasing the offended doctor.

"Fine," Rob agreed with a small huff, picking up her phone. "I'll text Lynn and tell her to bring him to my office in a week for a follow-up appointment." She tapped her phone screen. "I'd text Harry, but knowing him, he'd ignore it and try to remove the stitches himself."

"Yes, he would," Rosalie agreed with a deep nod.

"Hey! It's three of my favourite people." Max beamed as she approached their table. "My invitation must have gotten lost in the mail," she teased.

Gucci was so excited and in such a rush to greet his Aunt Max that he caught his back paw on his water bowl and flipped it over, spilling the contents all over the sidewalk. But he didn't let that stop him! He scurried out from under the table, wagging his quill-like tail, yelping with glee, and pawing her shins.

Max crouched down to pet her favourite terrier and scratched his neck under his collar as he bounced on his hind legs, trying to cover her face with kisses.

"It's an impromptu gathering," Rosalie explained. "But now that you're here, we insist you join us!"

"I'd love to," Max said with a sigh. "But I'm here on police business." She stood up, gesturing to her police uniform.

"What kind of police business?" Rosalie asked.

"The coffee and donut kind," Rob joked.

"Haha," Max replied. "The murder kind, actually. But I might grab a coffee and cruller to go. May as well, since I'm here."

"You're here about Leila's murder?" Karla asked.

Max nodded. "I'm showing Leila's photo around town." She pulled out her phone and flashed them a post-mortem photo of Leila's head and shoulders.

Aside from being too pale, Leila looked like she was sleeping. The photo included her distinctive tattoos, which should help jog some memories if anyone saw her before she died. "We could really use a lead." Max's voice was heavy with defeat. "Her loved ones must be worried sick by now. We need to identify her, so we can contact them."

"There still haven't been any missing persons reports matching her description?" Rob asked.

Max shook her head. "But the clerk who checked her in at The Seascape Hotel contacted us. He remembered a couple of things that he forgot when we interviewed him."

"Like what?" Karla rested her chin on her hand, giving Max her full attention.

Rosalie not-so-discreetly dropped another piece of lemon biscotti under the table. Gucci forgot all about his Aunt Max and scampered toward the forbidden treat.

"He gave us a good lead," Max started. "Dad is following up on it now."

"What lead?" Karla urged.

"According to the clerk, when Leila checked in, she told him that her boyfriend wasn't expecting her until the next day, but she wanted to surprise him, so she came to Bellbrook a day early," Max explained. "Also, Leila requested a second key for her room. She asked the clerk to keep the second key at the front desk in case her boyfriend showed up at the hotel before she got back from Shearlock Combs. She told him she was going to text her boyfriend from the salon and tell him to meet her at the hotel. The clerk said she was excited to see her boyfriend's reaction to her early arrival."

"Isn't it odd that the hotel clerk forgot all this when you questioned him?" Rob wondered.

"Not really," Max replied. "Most people don't have regular interactions with the police. Especially not because of something as serious as a murder investigation. He's young, he's new at his job, he was probably overwhelmed when we interviewed him the first time. This is one of the reasons we do multiple interviews."

"Did her boyfriend pick up the key?" Karla asked.

"No," Max replied. "The clerk was tidying up the registration desk this morning and came across the second key. It triggered his memory about her early arrival and the second key."

"Either Leila didn't call her boyfriend from the salon like she told the clerk, or she did phone him but he never showed up at the hotel because he knew Leila was dead, and he wouldn't need the key," Karla suggested.

"If he didn't know Leila was dead, wouldn't he have reported her missing when she didn't show up in Bellbrook, and he didn't hear from her?" Rosalie asked.

"Good point, Rosalie," Max said.

"Did Leila tell the hotel clerk her boyfriend's name?" Karla asked.

They all leaned in toward Max, eager to hear the answer.

"Yes," Max replied. "She said his name was Walter Crowfoot.

"Water Crowfoot?" Rosalie asked, scrunching up her face and cupping her ear as though she had misheard.

"No, Rosalie," Max said. "Walter Crowfoot. Walter." She stressed the L in Walter.

"Oh, that makes more sense." Rosalie nodded. "I thought you said Water Crowfoot, you know like the plant?"

"What plant?" Karla asked.

"Water Crowfoot is a type of buttercup that grows near water. It's a member of the Ranunculaceae family."

"Ranunculaceae?" Karla rolled the word around her tongue like a hard candy. She squeezed her eyes shut, wracking her brain to remember where she had heard that word recently.

"I don't know of any Crowfoots in Bellbrook," Rosalie said.

"Us either," Max replied, referring to the Bellbrook Police Department. "There are a few Walters, but none with the surname Crowfoot. We don't even have a Walter whose last name starts with C."

"How about The Aquaholic?" Rob asked, looking back and forth from Karla to Max.

Karla and Max shook their heads.

"I haven't met any Walters," Karla replied. "But I

haven't met the entire crew. It's shocking how many people it takes to keep a mega yacht afloat."

"There's no one on the yacht called Walter. Nobody with the surname Crowfoot, and nobody with the initials WC," Max added. "Dad and I believe finding Walter Crowfoot is the key to uncovering Leila's identity and solving her murder." She sighed and glanced in the cafe window. "I'd love to stay and chat, ladies, but I should go inside and show this photo to The Posers. If anyone saw Leila in Bellbrook before she died, it would be them," Max said.

"Yes, it would," Rosalie agreed.

"Do we know anything else about Leila's boyfriend?" Rob asked, after Max disappeared inside Déjà Brew.

"She talked about him at length with Lynn at the salon," Rosalie said.

"But she didn't tell Lynn any identifying information," Karla clarified. "According to Lynn, Leila said her boyfriend's job requires him to travel a lot, and he has a sensitive job in a secure environment."

"And Leila also told Lynn that she only sees her boyfriend every few weeks when he flies her to whichever town he's in," Rosalie added. "She said they have to keep a low profile when they're together because of his job, so they don't go out much."

Rob crossed her arms in front of her chest and tilted her head, dubious. "From what you describe, I'd say that Leila's boyfriend is either super famous and avoiding being seen in public with her, or he's married." She shrugged with her palms facing the sky. "And there aren't a lot of famous guys in Bellbrook, but there are a lot of married ones."

Karla and Rosalie looked at each other, mouths agape. Neither could believe they hadn't come to the same conclusion.

As far as Karla was aware, none of the suspects were married, but there was one who was certainly famous and travelled a lot with his social-media-celebrity fiancée.

Gucci panted at Karla's feet, distracting her from her thoughts about Leila's murder. She reached under the table and picked up the overturned water bowl. "I'll be right back," she said, standing up. "Gooch needs water." She shot Rosalie a sideways glance and grinned. "I think the biscotti is making him thirsty."

Rosalie said nothing, pretending not to hear Karla, and sipped her coffee.

TWENTY-THREE

MARIGOLDGATE

STANDING IN LINE, Karla's brain replayed Rob's revelation that Leila's boyfriend-slash-potential murderer might have been in a committed relationship with someone other than Leila. In hindsight, Rob was right. His actions, as Leila described them, seemed like the behaviour of someone who had something to hide. Something like a committed partner who had no clue what he was up to.

Was Ben Underwood Leila's boyfriend? Was Leila tired of meeting Ben for short, infrequent secret rendezvous? Maybe she threatened to expose their relationship, causing Ben to panic and kill her. Or maybe Leila confronted Saskia, and she killed Leila to stop the affair from becoming public knowledge, which would destroy her reputation and ruin her upcoming wedding. Maybe Ben and Saskia killed Leila together, and now they're keeping a deadly secret. But if that was the case, surely Saskia would have given Ben an alibi, right? Ben initially told the police that he was with Saskia the entire time Leila was aboard The Aquaholic, but Saskia told the police that she was alone in her cabin. Why would Saskia admit she had no alibi if she was guilty?

Karla stepped out of line and joined Max, who was showing Leila's photo to The Posers at a table near the window. She positioned herself where Max could see her. They exchanged small smiles. Karla stayed far enough away not to interfere in their conversation but close enough to eavesdrop.

"Yeah, I remember her." The brunette ponytail nodded at the image on Max's phone.

"Me too," said the reverse bob, looking over Max's shoulder.

"She was at Shearlock Combs the other morning," added the pixie cut, pointing to the salon across the street. "She was in there a while but came out looking exactly the same, so I don't think she had her hair done."

"You're very observant," Max praised the woman's observation skills. "She had her nails done."

The pixie cut smiled proudly.

"I figured she was a tourist," volunteered the brunette ponytail. "I didn't recognize her as a local, and she looked really happy." She smiled. "She was smiling and had a bounce in her step."

The reverse bob and pixie cut nodded in agreement.

Max put away her phone and pulled out her trusty notepad and pen. "Did you notice anything else about her?"

"Something caught her attention," said the reverse bob. "Remember?" She nudged the brunette ponytail. "She was smiling and happy, then all of a sudden, she froze."

"Oh, yeah," agreed the brunette ponytail. "She stopped dead in her tracks, and the cheerful expression disappeared from her face."

"It was like she suddenly remembered that she'd left the stove on, or she saw something she couldn't believe," added the pixie cut.

"We assumed she saw The Aquaholic for the first time. It's shockingly huge when you first see it," said the brunette ponytail.

"It had only arrived the day before," added the reverse bob. "Lots of people came to the waterfront that day to gawk at it."

"Did she speak to anyone?" Max asked.

"Not that we noticed," replied the pixie cut while all three of them shook their heads.

"Did you notice which way she went when she left the salon?" Max asked.

"I can't remember," the brunette ponytail giggled. Then the other two started giggling with her.

"We got distracted," explained the pixie cut. "That handsome captain from The Aquaholic showed up."

"He was outside," said the reverse bob. "Right

there." She pointed out the window at the sidewalk. "In full uniform." She waggled her eyebrows. "He stopped near the trash can and made eye contact with us through the window. He smiled right at us."

They giggled again, poking and nudging each other like giddy school girls.

"So, you lost track of Leila because you were swooning over Captain Peterson?" Max asked.

"He winked at us," gushed the pixie cut. "And his smile! It was hard to notice anything else."

Max closed her notebook with a sigh.

"Then he came inside and ordered a doppio and a cup of ice water to go," added the reverse bob. "On his way out, he tipped his cap, smiled, and said, 'G'day, ladies,' in the hottest accent we've ever heard."

"If it weren't for the giant wedding ring on his finger, I would've followed him all the way back to his yacht," cooed the brunette ponytail, then she let out a low purr, which encouraged her friends to break into a new fit of giggles.

Karla looked back at the line. It was longer now. She found a table, dropped herself into the chair, and set the Déjà Brew branded water bowl on the small bistro table. She watched as Max thanked The Posers and asked them to contact her should they remember anything else about Leila.

Max slipped behind the counter and showed the photo to the baristas, who stopped taking orders and making drinks just long enough to look at the photo and shake their heads. Max thanked them and quietly left Déjà Brew through the back door.

Ranunculaceae. Karla heard the word inside her head in Rosalie's voice. *Ranunculus,* this time it was Lynn's voice echoing through her mind. Lynn had mentioned ranunculuses yesterday morning when Karla had accused her of flirting with Captain Peterson. Ranunculaceae and ranunculuses. The words were too similar to be a coincidence. They must have had similar meanings, right? Karla unlocked her phone to search for the two similar sounding words on the internet.

"There you are!" Rob's voice brought Karla back to the here and now. "What's taking you so long?"

"Sorry," Karla said, locking her phone and picking up the empty water bowl. "I gave up my place in line to eavesdrop on Max's conversation with The Posers. When they finished, the line was so long, I sat down to wait a minute. Gucci must be thirsty." She motioned to stand up. "I'll get back in line."

"There's no point now," Rob said. "Rosalie left to walk to her gardening club meeting. She took Gucci with her and said she would get him a bowl of water when they get there." Rob sat in the chair across from Karla. "She said you would be OK with her taking Gucci to the Petal Pushers meeting. She said he goes all the time?"

"He does," Karla confirmed, still distracted by Ranunculaceae and the new information Max had learned from the hotel clerk.

"Did you know Gucci is the Petal Pushers mascot?" Rob asked.

Karla nodded. "He's been their mascot for a few months now."

"I didn't know gardening clubs had mascots."

"Me neither," Karla admitted. "Not until Rosalie told me the Petal Pushers had voted unanimously to make Gucci their new mascot."

"Why Gucci?" Rob asked.

"He fits into the old mascot's shirt," Karla replied.

"Old mascot?" Rob's face made it clear she had not heard about Marigoldgate.

"Mrs. Baumgartner's cat, Tabbytha," Karla explained. "Tabbytha lost her job as mascot because she ate Mr. Marshall's prize-winning marigolds. Mrs. Baumgartner's insisted that it couldn't have been Tabbytha because, according to her, Tabbytha hates marigolds."

"They fired Tabbytha without proof?"

"It was a big scandal," Karla told her. "I can't believe you haven't heard about Marigoldgate. It was all Rosalie talked about for weeks. Half the Petal Pushers believed Mrs. Baumgartner and supported Tabbytha. The other half supported Mr. Marshall, believing that Tabbytha ate his prize-winning marigolds as revenge because Mrs. Baumgartner's marigolds won second place behind Mr. Marshall's. It turned out Mr. Marshall caught the crime on his doorbell camera, but a few of the Petal Pushers think someone manipulated the footage."

"Wild," Rob said, shaking her head. "Only in Bellbrook."

"Well, since Gucci's gone to his garden club meeting, I'll return this dog bowl to the barista behind the counter."

They got up, and Karla walked over to the counter to hand in the bowl. Then she remembered she was about to search the internet before Rob distracted her and pulled out her phone again.

"Do you know how to spell ranunculus?" Karla asked as they left the cafe.

Rob sounded out the word, and between them, they figured out how to spell the uncommon word.

Gasp! Karla froze. The words on the screen left her motionless and speechless.

"What's wrong?" Rob asked.

Karla tilted her phone so Rob could see it. "I know who killed Leila."

ROB ENDED the call and put her phone on her lap. "Max said to wait for the police and instructed us not to confront the suspect without them."

"And she'll dig out Leila's ID and bring it with her?" Karla steered the car toward the marina.

"If it's there," Rob replied. "She sounded skeptical

that she'd find Leila's ID where you suspect the killer hid it. She said if you're right, the killer is more arrogant than she and Dean gave them credit for.

"The killer is arrogant, all right!" Karla nodded. "If I'm wrong, and Max doesn't find it, she'll get the satisfaction of saying, 'I told you so,'" Karla said. "She loves to do that, so she wins either way."

"Are you sure about this, Karla?" Rob's tone was serious. "Accusing someone of murder is a big deal. If it turns out you're wrong, you can't just take it back and expect them to forget all about it."

"Did you listen to the evidence?" For the second time, Karla explained to Rob how each piece of evidence pointed to one specific person.

"I agree with you," Rob said, "but most of the evidence is circumstantial. If you accuse them of murder, and it turns out they didn't kill Leila, or there isn't enough concrete evidence to convict them, it could cost you a client and your reputation. Not to mention, it would kibosh the celebrity wedding of the year that's supposed to reinvigorate Bellcroft as a world-class event venue and benefit almost every business in town."

"What choice do I have?" Karla asked. "I can't stand by and do nothing while a killer gets away with murder!"

"You could let the police handle it," Rob suggested. "Max said the police would only need a day or two to confirm your theory. Then, they can arrest the suspect, confront them with the evidence, and charge them with Leila's murder."

"In the meantime, there's nothing stopping the killer from realizing the police are onto them and making a run for it. Do you know how far someone with their resources and knowledge can get in one or two days?" It was a rhetorical question. "Far. The opposite side of the world. Somewhere with no extradition laws."

TWENTY-FOUR

BZZZ... TRY AGAIN

THEY ARRIVED AT THE MARINA, and Karla reversed the car into a parking spot. She turned off the engine, unbuckled her seatbelt, and motioned to get out of the vehicle.

"Hold on," Rob raised her hand in a stop motion. "Let's wait for the police." Karla opened her mouth to protest, but Rob continued. "We have an unobstructed view of The Aquaholic from here. If anyone leaves the yacht, we'll see them," she argued.

"Fine," Karla agreed. "But if the police aren't here in ten minutes, I'm calling Damien and asking him to send a yacht tender to pick me up. You can wait here for the police."

"I'm not letting you board that ship and confront a killer by yourself," Rob protested.

The familiar royal-blue Maserati cruised into the parking lot and parked a few spots away.

"There's my dream car," Rob whispered, forgetting about their difference of opinion.

"It's sleek," Karla commented. "And very fast when Caitlin is behind the wheel."

The passenger door opened, and Saskia got out of the car. Using the front-facing camera on her phone, she checked her makeup and touched up her hair.

Ben got out of the driver's side.

They laughed and flirted as Saskia directed Ben to lean against the sports car with his arms spread out on either side. He crossed his ankles and smiled while she snapped a few photos with her phone, then they switched. Saskia handed Ben her phone, sat on the hood of the car, crossed her long, slender legs, turned her head toward the ocean, closed her eyes, and tilted her face toward the sky while Ben snapped photos of her.

A black electric SUV pulled up. The bald, stone-faced security guard who had accompanied Ben and Saskia to Bellcroft the day before got out of the front passenger side and opened the back door. He stood at attention while Damien and Caitlin exited the vehicle.

"We might not have to go to them," Karla commented. "It looks like they're coming to us."

"What if they catch us staring at them?" Rob whispered.

"They won't," Karla replied. "They don't know what my car looks like. It's been in the shop since before they arrived in Bellbrook."

Damien, Caitlin, Saskia, and Ben gathered in the parking lot, chatting and smiling.

Damien struck a match on the bottom of his loafer and proceeded to toast a fresh cigar.

Caitlin checked the time on her watch and said something to the others while jerking her head toward the nearby dock. The group started moving in that direction.

"This must be their lift back to the yacht," Rob said, pointing her chin at the speedboat that had appeared in front of the yacht and was speeding toward shore.

"Then it's our lift too." Karla opened the door and jumped out of the car before Rob could convince her otherwise. "Damien," she called, knowing the entire group would stop if he did. "Wait up!" She jogged toward them with Rob running to catch up.

"Karla! What a lovely surprise," Damien said as she approached the group. "What brings you here? Do we have a meeting I've forgotten about?"

Karla opened her mouth to reply.

"O. M. G.!" Saskia declared, interrupting before Karla could utter a syllable. "We just saw Gucci! He was sooo cute! He was wearing a little T-shirt that said, Petal Pushers, with a cartoon sunflower on it." She reached over and touched Karla's forearm. "He was so adorable. I just had to take a picture! I'll send it to you." Saskia turned her attention to her phone.

"We just enjoyed a late lunch at your local pub."

Damien squeezed his brows together and looked at Caitlin. "What was the name of that pub again?"

"The Pavlovian," Caitlin replied, then smiled at Karla. "Such a cozy, friendly little establishment."

"We ate outside," Damien continued. "The proprietor called it the beer garden." He puffed his cigar.

"Wonderful food," Caitlin commented. "Fabulous service and such a nice ambience."

When did you all become so talkative?

"I would've stayed longer and had another beer or two," Damien added. "But a bunch of people in Petal Pushers shirts showed up. They were having a loud and heated discussion about a gardening emergency, of all things." Damien chuckled. "Apparently, someone named Harry injured his hand, and the rest of them are fixing to keep his garden in tip-top shape until he gets better." He puffed his cigar and smoke billowed above them. "Sounded like a big garden."

"It was very dramatic," Saskia commented. "Someone named Mr. Marshall refused to sit near someone named Mrs. Baumgartner. Apparently, he was mad at her cat? Anyway, they had to rearrange the whole table. Twice. It was like musical chairs."

"Small town drama," Karla said with a smile.

"When Gucci showed up, it was game over for Ben," Damien said with an eye roll.

"The lady who brought Gucci was super sweet and understanding when she saw how panicked Ben was.

She kept Gucci on his leash and everything, but Ben couldn't handle being so close to a dog."

"Who expects to run into a dog at a restaurant?" Ben asked in his own defence. "He took me by surprise."

Karla nodded, hoping Gucci's sudden appearance in the Pavlovian's beer garden didn't set back his exposure therapy, and trying to get a word in edgewise.

"We decided it would be best to leave," Caitlin explained, giving Karla a knowing eyebrow raise. "By the way, how's your car? All fixed?"

"It's good," Karla replied. "It's over there." She gestured vaguely behind her. "The reaso—"

"I hope you and Dr. Mayhew will join us on the yacht," Damien interrupted, and Karla wondered if she would ever speak a complete sentence again without one of them cutting her off.

"Actually, I don't think it's a good idea for any of us to return to the yacht right now," Karla began.

"Poppycock!" Damien declared before she could finish her thought. "We won't take no for an answer. We insist that you and Dr. Mayhew join us for drinks on the upper deck." Damien waved the cigar as he gesticulated with his hands. "It will give us a chance to discuss your new position." He winked and returned the stogie to his mouth.

"New position?" Rob asked.

"Didn't Karla tell you?" Damien asked, clenching

the cigar in his teeth. "I've offered her the opportunity of a lifetime."

"You never mentioned it," Rob muttered to Karla, confused.

The yacht tender had arrived at the dock. Captain Peterson used ropes to moor the boat, then hopped off, hoisting a backpack over his shoulder and pulling a dark, wheeled suitcase behind him. He was wearing civilian clothes and a baseball cap instead of his uniform.

"Peterson, what's going on?" Damien demanded upon seeing his ship's captain hurrying toward them with packed bags and civilian attire.

"Family emergency, sir," Captain Peterson explained. "I've already sent for a freelance captain to replace me. He'll arrive tomorrow. In the meantime, the first mate is in charge, and you or Ben can drive yourselves back to the yacht." He tossed a keychain with a triangular key at Ben, who caught it with ease.

"Is there anything we can do, Henry?" Caitlin asked, her face full of concern.

"No, thank you." Captain Peterson nodded. "I need to get to the airport. I have a plane to catch."

"Get in the SUV," Damien instructed. "My driver will take you."

"Thank you, sir." Captain Peterson nodded and continued walking. "I'll be in touch as soon as I can."

The group parted down the middle, creating a direct path between Captain Peterson and the waiting SUV.

As soon as Captain Peterson breezed past Karla, she said, "Walter!"

He stopped. There was a pause before he turned and glared at her with narrowed eyes. "What did you call me?"

"How did you know I meant you?"

He glanced around at the confused faces, then relaxed his shoulders, allowing his backpack to slide to the ground. He pushed the rolling suitcase toward the security guard and bolted.

"Stop him!" Rob shouted.

The security guard sprang into action and scaled the suitcase Captain Peterson had shoved in his way.

Ben gave chase too, leaping in front of the accomplished yachtsman and blocking his getaway, allowing the security guard to catch up and lunge at him. The large bodyguard nabbed the attempted escapee and dragged him back toward the SUV. He twisted Captain Peterson's arm behind his back to stop him from trying to squirm out of his grasp.

"Peterson, why did Karla call you Walter?" Damien asked his soon-to-be-former captain.

"I don't know, sir," Captain Peterson replied. "You'd have to ask her."

Karla felt the weight of everyone's stares on her.

"Walter is Captain Peterson's alias," she explained, without breaking eye contact with the suspected killer. "Walter Crowfoot. At least, that's what you told Leila your name was, right?"

"I don't know what you're talking about," Captain Peterson claimed. "I've never heard that name before."

Karla turned to the group of confused onlookers. "Captain Peterson was Leila's boyfriend," she revealed. "Every few weeks, he would fly her into a town near where The Aquaholic was anchored and sneak away to meet her for secret trysts."

"She has no clue what she's talking about," Captain Peterson said with an awkward chuckle. "I'm a happily married man. I think your concierge might be a few sandwiches short of a picnic, sir."

Damien's face was expressionless. He was giving nothing away. "Keep talking Karla."

"Leila didn't know you were married, did she?"

Captain Peterson said nothing, scowling at her.

"I bet she didn't even know you worked on The Aquaholic, did she?"

Still no reaction from the alleged murderer.

"Two days ago, Leila arrived in Bellbrook earlier than you had expected. She had missed you since your last rendezvous, and she wanted to surprise you, so she came to town a day early. She checked in at the hotel, then visited Shearlock Combs for a manicure and pedicure because she wanted to look her absolute best for you. She was going to text you on your secret burner phone and ask you to meet her at the hotel, but before she did, she saw you. You were outside Déjà Brew just as Leila left Shearlock Combs. She recognized you despite your uniform, and she saw your wedding ring.

The jig was up. Leila realized you were married, and she'd figured out you were a liar."

"You have an active imagination, I'll give you that," Captain Peterson said with a chuckle. "Surely you don't believe this woman's inane ramblings, Mr. Casey?"

Two police cruisers squealed into opposite sides of the parking lot, blocking the entrance and exit. Max hopped out of one police car, and Dean got out of the other. There were more sirens in the distance. Backup.

"You're just in time," Captain Peterson shouted, struggling against the large security officer who was restraining him. "Thank goodness you're here. This man is holding me against my will, and this crazy woman is making up unbelievable stories about me and accusing me of murder!"

"No one has accused you of murder," Caitlin pointed out. "At least, not yet." She looked at Karla and nodded for her to continue.

"After Leila realized you were an adulterous liar, she set out to confront you. She returned to the hotel, gathered her belongings, and used fake credentials to sneak aboard The Aquaholic. She bided her time, even ordering lunch from the yacht kitchen. Terrified that someone would realize Leila was there for you, and that she would expose your dirty secret, you killed her. We discovered her body before you finished removing her luggage and other belongings from the yacht and disposing of them."

Max approached the bodyguard and relieved him of

his detainee, slapping handcuffs on Captain Peterson, and thanking the security officer for restraining him until the police arrived.

"Where did you get the name Walter Crowfoot?" asked Captain Peterson.

"Leila asked the hotel clerk to keep a second room key at the front desk for her boyfriend to pick up. She told the clerk her boyfriend's name was Walter Crowfoot. You told Lynn that your wife's favourite flowers were ranunculuses and mentioned that you have a garden full of them at home. You gave her the impression that you had expert knowledge of them. Later, my friend Rosalie mentioned a plant called Water Crowfoot that was part of the Ranunculaceae family."

"Oooh, you should have chosen a more random name," Saskia criticized, holding her phone in such a way that Karla wondered if she was recording the interaction.

"The last clue was your wedding ring," Karla revealed. "It's a gorgeous ring, and I found it mesmerizing, but I couldn't figure out why. At first, I thought it was because it was shiny and interesting to look at, but then I realized it wasn't your ring that mesmerized me, it was your finger." She held up her left hand and wiggled her ring finger. "There's no tan line under your wedding ring. You claim to remove your ring hardly ever, yet you have no tan line at all. Despite being one of the most tanned people I've met. Either you remove your ring more often than you claim, or you cover the tan line with self-tanner or something. Either way, you went out of your way to appear unmarried."

"This is all circumstantial." Captain Peterson spat when he spoke. "You can't prove anything!" He scoffed. "The police don't even know the dead woman's name. If she and I were contacting each other with burner phones, as you claim, where's my burner phone? Hmmm?" he challenged.

"Right here," Dean replied, holding up a sealed evidence bag. "Along with Leila Grant's passport and the contents of her wallet. Thank you by the way"—he tipped his head to the captain—"for not bothering to delete the selfies of you and Leila from your burner phone. You should have erased the phone before you tossed it. Rookie mistake. Those photos, combined with the intimate texts between you and Leila, will make it hard for you to deny your relationship with the deceased." He placed the bag on the roof of his patrol car. "I bet when we process these, we'll find your fingerprints all over them, won't we?"

The colour drained from Captain Peterson's face, and he swallowed hard, shaking his head and glowering at the evidence bag in Dean's hand.

"Karla and I watched you toss an old crumpled up paper bag into the garbage can outside Déjà Brew when you were talking to Lynn yesterday," Rob explained.

"You hadn't visited the cafe yet for your usual order,

so we figured you weren't tossing the garbage from your morning coffee," Karla continued. "We suspect you hid Leila's ID and your burner phone in her suitcase, the one you hid in the yacht tender, then retrieved it the next morning and disposed of it in a public garbage can, where the police wouldn't be likely to search."

"What do you have to say for yourself, Peterson?" Damien asked.

"Nothing, sir. It's all lies."

"Fair enough," Damien agreed, nodding. "Caitlin, get Peterson's wife on the phone. Maybe she can clear up a few details for us."

Caitlin nodded and unlocked her phone. "Yes, Damien."

"No!" Captain Peterson shouted. "Please don't call my wife."

"Then tell us what happened, Peterson."

"Fine, I had an affair with Leila Grant," Captain Peterson admitted, "but I didn't kill her."

"Was her death an accident?" Max asked.

"I don't know how she died," Captain Peterson replied. "She used the phone in the cabin to contact the quarterdeck. I answered the call. I couldn't believe my ears. How did she get on the yacht, I wondered? Who else knew she was here? She gave me fifteen minutes to get to her cabin, or she would call my wife and tell her everything, then she would announce it through the yacht's intercom system."

"What happened when you got there?" Caitlin asked.

"Nothing," Captain Peterson replied, shaking his head. "When I arrived, Leila was already dead. She was floating in the bathtub. There was a half-eaten salad in the cabin. She could've choked," he suggested, stammering and grasping for each word. "Or maybe she took her own life to get back at me."

"*Bzzz,*" Rob made a game show buzzer sound. "Wrong answer. Try again."

"I don't know what more you want me to say?!" Captain Peterson protested, sputtering his words and blinking from the beads of sweat that were dripping into his eyes. "I didn't kill her. I might be an adulterer, but I'm not a murderer." He fumbled a few incoherent words and shook his head, searching for what to say next. "Do you really think I'm so heartless that I would smother someone to death with a pillow, then cover up my crime by leaving her in a tub of water?"

"*Ding, ding, ding,*" Rob did her best imitation of a bell. "Right answer."

There it was. The holdback. Aside from Rob, the police, and Karla, only Leila's killer knew how she died.

"Henry Peterson, you're under arrest for the murder of...."

"Suffocate?"

"I thought she drowned?"

"She didn't die in the bathtub?"

"He smothered her?"

Damien, Caitlin, Saskia, and Ben's shocked disbelief drowned out Max's voice as she arrested Captain Peterson, reading him his rights and marching him to her patrol car.

TWENTY-FIVE

FLOTSAM AND JETSAM

THREE DAYS after the arrest

Karla inhaled a lungful of salty sea air and fixed her eyes on the hazy grey-blue horizon line in the distance, watching the tiny white dot as it shrank into non-existence.

"It's hard to believe that tiny speck is a cruise ship-sized yacht," she commented.

"One phone call to Damien Casey, and that cruise ship-sized yacht could be your and Gucci's new home," Rob said, watching Gucci sniff a caterpillar that was inching along the wooden dock. "How did Damien react when you declined his offer?"

"He was disappointed but understanding," Karla replied. "He countered by offering me the flexibility to work for him on a project-by-project basis. I told him I would think about it and let him know when he comes back to Bellbrook for Saskia and Ben's wedding. But I already know the answer will be no."

Saskia had been right when she warned Karla that saying no to Damien would only make him more persistent.

Karla explained to Damien that she had no desire to work in politics. Heck, she had trouble paying attention to Bellbrook's low-stakes, small-town politics, or even the drama within The Petal Pushers, never mind the high stakes political games Damien Casey played. Also, she was averse to using her lie detection ability for financial gain.

"Have you heard from Caitlin?" Rob asked. "How was her flight?"

"She landed early this morning," Karla said. "She's nervous and excited to spend time with her sister, niece, and nephew again."

After Captain Peterson's arrest, they returned to the yacht, and Caitlin sat down with Damien and confessed her feelings for him. She told Karla he was taken aback but did not dismiss the possibility that someday they could be more than friends and colleagues. He told Caitlin he needed time to sort out his feelings.

Then she called her sister and started the process of reconciling their relationship. Caitlin said her sister was so happy to hear from her that they cried together on the phone. Caitlin hadn't taken time off work in years. Damien owed her months of paid vacation time, and she was using a good chunk of it before Saskia and

Damien's wedding. She planned to spend her time away from her career getting to know her family again and getting to know herself again. To rediscover the person she was before she reinvented herself in the image of Damien's ideal partner.

Karla could tell Damien was already missing Caitlin and suspected her absence might make his heart grow fonder. Though part of her wondered if Caitlin would still feel the same about Damien after her time away.

"Can you text Caitlin for me?" Rob asked. "Tell her I said thank you for letting me drive the Maserati when we dropped her off at the airport yesterday. She made one of my dreams come true."

"Sure," Karla agreed as they meandered along the waterfront. "When Caitlin texted earlier, she said to tell you the car rental place is picking up the Maserati at six o'clock tonight, so you can drive it until then, but it has to be back in the marina parking lot by six p.m."

"Really?!" Rob's brown eyes lit up, and her smile was wide. "I'll be able to drive it to pick up Josie from her dad's place. She already thinks I'm the coolest mom in the world because of my viral social media sound bites. I didn't even know viral sound bites were a thing."

During Captain Peterson's confession, Karla had noticed Saskia's cell phone and wondered if Saskia was recording the confrontation. She wasn't. Saskia didn't record the confession, she livestreamed it. Millions of Saskians all over the world watched the murderer's confession in real time. Needless to say, it went viral; everything Saskia does goes viral.

It turned out Captain Peterson's wife was a Saskian. Her phone notified her when Saskia's livestream started. According to Max, Mrs. Peterson was at work, sitting in her office when she tuned into the livestream just in time to watch her handcuffed husband say, "Fine, I had an affair with Leila Grant, but I didn't kill her." She watched the rest of the confession and later confirmed to Max that there was no emergency at home. It was Mrs. Peterson's opinion that Captain Peterson wasn't coming home at all but was attempting to evade the long arm of the law. The day after his arrest, she found a charge on their joint credit card for a one-way ticket to Venezuela.

In his formal statement, Captain Peterson claimed he had suspected the police were closing in on him, and his days as a free man were about to come to an end, so he tried to make a run for it while the family was having lunch at The Pavlovian. But they came back early and foiled his escape, thanks to The Petal Pushers, Gucci, and Ben's cynophobia.

Besides Captain Peterson's confession being featured by television and internet news outlets across the globe, Saskians isolated Rob's game show buzzer and game show bell imitations, turning them into a viral social media trend. Rob's voice was trending in thirty-second videos on every social media platform.

"If Josie thinks you're cool now, wait until you roll

up in the Maserati and tell her you've met Saskia Casey," Karla teased.

"I plan to enjoy every second," Rob admitted. "It's temporary. By this time next week, the world will have moved on to the next viral trend, and I'll go back to being a boring mom who wears scrubs and makes her eat vegetables."

"You could never be a boring mom," Karla reassured her best friend.

"I have a telephone appointment later today with Leila's family," Rob revealed. "Dean arranged it. They have questions about how she died."

"That doesn't sound like a fun call," Karla sympathized. "Would you like me to be there?"

"I was thinking of asking Lynn to be there. She had more interaction with Leila while she was in Bellbrook than anyone. Other than Captain Peterson, I mean. The family might want to talk to her. She could tell them about their last conversation at Shearlock Combs."

"I'm sure Lynn would do that for them."

Rob's phone chimed, and she checked the screen. "Harry," she said with a sigh.

"Again?" Karla asked. "What does he want now?"

"He wants me to remove his stitches," Rob replied. "He says his hand is itchy, and the stitches limit his ability to do anything."

"He's been asking you to remove his stitches since the day after he got them."

"I know," Rob said, shaking her head. "I keep telling

him they aren't ready yet, but he doesn't care. He hates sitting around watching the Petal Pushers putter in his gardens."

"Harry might complain about the Petal Pushers tending to Bellcroft's gardens, but he doesn't complain when they show up with Rosalie's homemade meals and treats," Karla pointed out.

"I don't think Harry's issue is with every member of the Petal Pushers," Rob revealed. "Apparently, Mr. Marshall took it upon himself to plant some of his prize-winning marigolds, prominently, in one of Harry's flower beds. Harry is not happy. He says they don't match the theme of that particular garden. Lynn told him to be nice, so he complimented the flowers, and now he's afraid Mr. Marshall will plant more marigolds. Yesterday, he mumbled something about how it would be a shame if Clancy developed a taste for them."

"I'd better talk to him. We don't need another Marigoldgate," Karla said, shaking her head. "There are still hurt feelings about the last one."

"Maybe Lynn knew what she was doing when she took Harry to the hospital for stitches instead of taking him to my office," Rob pondered aloud. "Maybe she knew he'd pester me every day to remove his stitches."

"You could be right," Karla agreed. "Lynn seems to know Harry better than most of us."

Rob looked at Karla. "Do you think Lynn and Harry will get together now that she's back in Bellbrook?"

Karla shrugged. "I don't know. They have a weird vibe. Sometimes they bicker like siblings, and other times I could swear they're flirting. If something is brewing there, I hope she doesn't break his heart by leaving."

"Where is Lynn?" Rob asked.

"She's researching puppies," Karla replied. "Ben has made such great progress with his exposure therapy that he wants to go ahead and surprise Saskia with a puppy on their wedding day. He gave Lynn a list of requirements, and she's searching shelters all over the country for their perfect dog."

"What breeds did he choose?" Rob asked.

"Small ones," Karla replied. "He can't handle anything bigger than Gucci." The little dog pricked up his ears and tilted his scruffy head at the sound of his name. "Ben came over to visit Gucci last night," Karla continued. "He told Saskia he was taking the Maserati out for one last drive, which wasn't a lie since he drove the Maserati to my place. His therapist was on the phone with him while I held Gucci on my lap. It took quite a while, but Ben got close enough to pet him and even let Gucci lick his hand."

Karla's phone chimed. "It's a notification from the bank," she said, scrunching up her face in confusion. "A money transfer from Damien." She opened the notification, and her eyes almost bugged out of her head when she saw the amount. "A lot of money." She looked at Rob. "But I didn't send him an invoice."

"Maybe it's a deposit toward Saskia and Ben's wedding." Rob shrugged one shoulder.

"Saskia's sponsors are paying for everything related to the wedding, including my consultation fee," Karla explained. "Damien must have sent this by mistake. I'll text him and let him know I'll transfer it back to him straight away." She opened the text messaging app, and her thumbs flew across the screen so fast they were a blur.

Soon after Karla hit send on her message to Damien, he replied.

"What did he say?" Rob asked when she heard Karla's phone chime.

"He insists it wasn't a mistake," Karla replied. "He says the money is a bonus. It's his way of thanking me for helping to solve Leila's murder, saving their reputations, and finding the perfect wedding venue for Saskia. He also says the money is a taste of the compensation I can expect should I decide to work for him."

Karla's phone chimed again.

"It's Damien again," she said. "He says it will offend him if I return the money." She sighed.

"I guess you'll have to keep it." Rob's voice was thick with mock sympathy.

"But it's too much," Karla objected, tilting her phone screen to show Rob the amount of Damien's bonus.

"Holy moly!" Rob blinked twice, and her eyes were

wide. "That'll help cover the costs of renovating Bellbrook."

"You're right," Karla agreed. "I can use it to payback some of the money Lynn and Harry invested." She gave Rob an impish grin. "Maybe we could solve a few more murders that earn a bonus and cover the cost of the entire renovation," she teased.

"Bite your tongue," Rob scolded. "The last thing Bellbrook needs is another murder. At this rate, Bellbrook will need a full-time coroner."

"Are you afraid another murder will interfere with your summer plans?" Karla asked with a laugh.

"Aren't you?" Rob rebutted.

Kind of, Karla thought to herself.

ABOUT THE AUTHOR

Reagan Davis is a pen name for the real author who lives in the suburbs of Toronto with her husband, two kids, and a menagerie of pets.

When she's not planning the perfect murder, she enjoys knitting, reading, eating too much chocolate, and drinking too much Diet Coke.

The author is an established knitwear designer who has contributed to many knitting books and magazines. I'd tell you her real name, but then I'd have to kill you. (Just kidding! Sort of.)

http://www.ReaganDavis.com/

ALSO BY REAGAN DAVIS

The Bellbrook Murder Mystery Series:

Ice Girls Finish Last

A Well Constructed Murder

Rage Before Beauty

Lost & Drowned

The Knitorious Murder Mystery Series:

Knit One Murder Two

Killer Cables

Murder & Merino

Twisted Stitches

Son of a Stitch

Crime Skein

Rest In Fleece

Life Crafter Death

In Stitchness and in Health

Bait & Stitch

Murder It Seams

Neigbourhood Swatch: A Knitorious Cozy Mystery Short
Story

Click here to sign up for Reagan Davis' email list to be
notified of new releases and special offers.

Follow Reagan Davis on Amazon

Follow Reagan Davis on Facebook, Bookbub, Goodreads, and Instagram

Made in the USA
Las Vegas, NV
30 March 2023

69896423R00152

COVID-19 und die Bedrohungen durch Pandemien

Wie sie entstehen und was wir dagegen tun müssen
Stefan H.E. Kaufmann